WON BY THE VISCOUNT

LEGENDARY LORDS OF THE TON

SUZANNA MEDEIROS

Legends and Love collide…

They are the men no woman can tame.
Some whisper about them. Others want to be them.
Known for their wealth, scandalous love affairs, and
the secrets that surround them.
They are the Legendary Lords of the ton.

WON BY THE VISCOUNT

A reckless wager. A scandalous bargain. A love neither of them saw coming.

I never should have accepted the baron's wager.
When he offered up a "rare family jewel" instead of
coin, I expected an heirloom and not his sister, Miss
Caroline Edwards, the diamond of the Season.

Honor demanded I walk away. Temptation made me stay.

Caroline is everything a gentleman should avoid—clever, independent, and entirely too irresistible. Desperate to escape an unwanted betrothal, she proposes a shocking bargain: if I pretend to court her, we can destroy her flawless reputation and set her free.

It should have been a harmless charade. But the more time I spend with Caroline—the stolen waltzes, the whispered laughter, the dangerous heat between us—the harder it becomes to remember which parts are pretend.

Now the stakes are far higher than I ever intended. Because the only thing more perilous than winning her... is losing her.

Perfect for readers who love *fake courtships, reluctant rogues,* and *clever heroines who upend every rule of Society, WON BY THE VISCOUNT* delivers a Regency romance full of wit, charm, and heart-stealing passion.

To learn about Suzanna Medeiros's future books,
you can sign up for her newsletter at:
suzannamedeiros.com/newsletter

There was something in his expression that should have warned me about what he was planning.

"Are we being watched?" he asked.

He made a quick turn around the edge of the dance floor, and I glanced at the people who were watching. It might have been my imagination, but they *all* appeared to be staring at us. Even the other couples who were dancing. I hadn't noticed before now because I'd been so caught up in Kendrick's larger-than-life presence. But now I could see the way the couples closest to us seemed to be straining to overhear our conversation.

I met his gaze again. "I thought the attention I attracted before tonight was excessive, but the way everyone is scrutinizing you…" I shook my head. "How do you stand it?"

He lifted one shoulder, the movement slight but noticeable under my hand. "It can be useful."

Then before I realized what he intended to do,

he danced me straight through the garden doors. The last sound I heard was the soft gasp of a matron who was staring at us, her mouth open in astonishment as we disappeared onto the balcony.

Copyright © 2025 by Saozinha Medeiros

WON BY THE VISCOUNT
First Digital Edition: October 2025
First Print Edition: October 2025
Edited by Red Adept Editing
ebook ISBN: 9781988223674
Paperback ISBN: 9781988223681

This is a work of fiction. Names, characters, places, and incidents either are the product of the author's imagination or are used fictitiously, and any resemblance to actual persons, living or dead, business establishments, events, or locales is entirely coincidental.

For Angelo and Daddy.
Love you both, always.

CHAPTER 1

VISCOUNT KENDRICK

JUNE 1820

The cards were in my favor tonight. I almost felt guilty for the man seated across from me who hadn't had the sense to fold. Honestly, I was doing him a service by pushing him to give up. Brag was not his game, and he was clearly out of his depth.

I raised the stakes. The air in the gaming room at King's was tense with expectation as people stopped to watch the two of us. The other players had long since tossed in their cards since my victory was all but certain. Only a fool would continue.

I could tell by the way Baron Weston's jaw tightened ever so slightly that he knew he was about to lose. But then he forced himself to relax and leaned forward. "Will you take something in lieu of money?"

I shouldn't have found it shocking that he was so stubborn. If he was in his cups, I'd deny his request. But as far as I'd seen, Weston hadn't had a drop to drink all night. I wasn't about to take his townhouse or be fooled into accepting a piece of property that turned out to be entailed and beyond my reach.

I leaned back in my chair. "That depends on what it is."

"A jewel," he said, a gleam in his eye. "A rare family jewel that is highly valued."

I watched him carefully, wondering which female family member he was about to deprive of a prized bauble. I should have denied his request. But the sly expression on Weston's face daring me to fold made me hesitate. If he was foolish enough to give away a family heirloom, perhaps this was a lesson he needed to learn.

Viscount Fairfax, who sat to my left, leaned in close. "I don't think you should agree." When I raised a brow, he lowered his voice and continued, "I thought you only accepted money."

I shrugged. "It's a jewel. I can sell it."

Fairfax's eyes narrowed. He looked at Weston then back at me. "I don't think you'll be able to sell this."

"Why? Because it might be a family heirloom?"

Fairfax's concern seemed unwarranted. "I'm not as soft-hearted as you. If the fool is willing to bet something that is precious to his family, it isn't my concern."

"I think you should listen to me on this," Fairfax said.

I couldn't understand why the man was being so squeamish about a jewel. "Are you still bitter that I've been trouncing you all evening?"

Fairfax raised his hands in surrender and leaned back in his chair. "Never say I didn't warn you."

I ignored him and met Weston's gaze. "What type of jewel?"

His expression was intense. "A diamond."

A few gasps from the spectators told me they knew something I didn't. Did his family possess a diamond valued so highly?

I nodded to the baron. If he wanted to lose it, I would give him that opportunity.

I motioned to one of the footmen standing at attention, and he handed Weston a piece of paper, a quill, and an inkpot to write the promissory note.

Weston scribbled a few words, signed the note with a flourish, then tossed it onto the large pile of coins between us.

"That is all I have, if you're thinking of raising again."

I shrugged. "No need."

I showed him my hand, grinning when Weston swore and tossed his cards face down on the table.

I signaled for the footman to collect the coins and stood. "Perhaps next time you should stop before you give away something you don't want to lose."

His eyes narrowed on me. I had the feeling he was about to say something, but he merely nodded. "Call on me tomorrow at one."

He turned, and I watched him leave.

Fairfax clapped me on the shoulder. "I don't think you should have done that." He plucked the promissory note from where it rested atop the collected coins and unfolded it. "I knew it," he said, shaking his head. He handed me the small paper.

I scanned the words.

To Viscount Kendrick:

As promised, I am giving you the rarest jewel I possess. The diamond of the season… Miss Caroline Edwards.

You may call on me tomorrow afternoon, and we can discuss this matter further.

—Baron Weston

I stared at the words for almost a full minute. "This can't be real."

I turned to Fairfax, who had wisely stepped back. He raised his hands in surrender. "I tried to tell you that you didn't want to accept his note."

"Did he actually…?" I couldn't say the words.

Rexford was going to be furious when he found out what had just transpired in his club.

Fairfax nodded. "He gave you his sister. The woman who refused to have a season last year and had to be forced to come to town this year. The woman every other man wants. Now she's yours."

I swore and stormed from the card room.

CHAPTER 2

MISS CAROLINE EDWARDS

Well past midday, my brother finally dragged himself out of bed, as was his custom. After escorting Aunt Augusta and me to a musicale yesterday evening, he'd disappeared for the rest of the night. I didn't particularly mind that he hadn't stayed, but I did worry about his gambling. Of late, he seemed to be heading to the gaming tables every night.

I would have been happier if he'd left me at home in Dorset, but Auntie had impressed upon him that I needed to be out in society this year. I'd managed to delay the ordeal last year, but my reprieve was over.

What alarmed me was the note he'd left saying he had a matter of great importance to discuss with me. As a result, I had spent the morning pacing and worrying.

Normally, I found great comfort in the library, but today, no book could ease my concern over my brother's need to speak to me. As soon as I heard his heavy footsteps in the hallway, I left the room. He was distracted at the best of times, and I wanted to get this conversation over with as soon as possible.

The sight of him already standing outside the library when I exited only increased my unease.

His expression was grave, and I tried to hold back my alarm. "Did something happen, Henry?" When he looked away, my dread grew. "Please tell me that everything is fine."

He inclined his head toward the drawing room. "We should sit down for this conversation."

I didn't know why we couldn't speak in the library, but I did what he asked and made my way down the hallway. He allowed me to precede him, which was troubling. My brother usually went out of his way to ignore me. Now he was being overly solicitous, which meant the news would likely upset or anger me.

"I need to talk to you about your future," he said when we entered the front room.

I stiffened. "I am in London, am I not? I am attending all the balls and plays Auntie has asked me to attend."

"And you are the diamond of the season." He smiled, but I could tell it was insincere.

I frowned, hating that title. I certainly wasn't the prettiest of the debutantes this year, and I was one year older than most. I suspected word had spread about my overly generous dowry. And given my blonde hair, blue eyes, and generous bosom, the suitors had been relentless. I detested every second of their attentions.

"You might not need to attend many more events," he continued.

I stared at my brother, and for a moment, my heart soared. But the unmistakable look of guilt on his face had my hopes crashing back to reality. "Tell me you haven't accepted a betrothal request without talking to me."

His gaze skittered away.

I took a deep breath and tried to hold back the anger threatening to take over. "Please tell me you haven't told Lord Penham I'll be marrying him."

Penham was my brother's closest friend, and he'd been a thorn in my side for years now. He and Henry were eight years older than me, so Penham had ignored me when we were young, something that had bothered me at the time. A few years ago, I began to notice that the way he looked at me had changed. It was now my turn to ignore *him*, but since we were in town for the season and I was on the marriage mart, his attention had become insufferable.

Henry had made it clear he wanted me to marry his friend, but I wanted nothing of the sort. If I was forced to choose this season, I would rather marry the oldest, most decrepit man—and there were several who fit that description attempting to woo me—than Penham. At least then I'd soon be widowed and free from unwanted attention.

He met my gaze. "I'm expecting a call, and your presence is required."

"Henry." I was pleading now, but I didn't care. "Please. I can't marry Lord Penham. You know I despise him."

He frowned. "You're overreacting. Penham

would be a wonderful husband. You would be lucky to have him."

"Henry—"

He let out an exasperated breath. "I'm not expecting Penham."

I sent up a silent thank you. But whom was Henry expecting if not Penham? I placed my hands on my hips and frowned at my brother. "What did you do? Does Aunt Augusta know?"

He winced. "She'll find out soon enough."

What was Henry going on about? For a moment, I worried this had to do with his gambling, but surely that wouldn't involve me. I took a step closer and softened my voice. "If you tell me what happened, I'll help you fix it."

There was a knock at the front door then, and Henry's shoulders slumped. "You should sit down for this. I expect you won't be happy."

I dropped onto the settee and folded my hands in my lap, dreading the disaster that was about to be revealed. But as long as Lord Penham wasn't calling, I could deal with whatever mess Henry had created.

Or at least I hoped so.

I tried to mask my tension. Perhaps Henry had

invited one of his acquaintances from King's, the club he'd been frequenting. But if so, whom?

There was a murmur of voices in the hallway, then the butler appeared just inside the drawing room and announced the caller.

Viscount Kendrick.

Henry was still standing, and I saw the way he stiffened when the butler departed and another man took his place.

A thrill of something surprising shot through me as I took in the devastatingly handsome man who bowed to my brother. He was tall—taller than Henry—and his hair was dark brown. When he turned to look at me, I was taken aback by his beauty. Sculpted features, full lips that should have looked ridiculous on a man but didn't, and deep-blue eyes.

It took me a moment to place the name. Viscount Kendrick was one of the Legendary Lords. Good heavens, I hadn't realized Henry moved in such scandalous circles. But then, King's was their club. I'd just assumed he didn't actually know any of the Legends. Apparently, I was wrong.

"How kind of you to call," my brother said, inclining his head.

Kendrick appeared amused as his gaze took in

the interior of the room before settling on me. "You didn't give me much choice last night. I'm here to discuss the payment of your debt."

Henry turned to face me. "Let me introduce you to my sister, Miss Caroline Edwards. Caroline, this is Viscount Kendrick."

I stood and dipped into a shallow curtsy. "It is a pleasure to meet you, my lord. What brings you here today?"

Kendrick's gaze moved between the two of us, and a knowing gleam lit his eyes. "You haven't told her."

Henry shrugged. "I was about to, but…"

Kendrick pulled out a pocket watch, looked at it, then met my brother's gaze. "I am on time. You've had all morning to speak to your sister."

Something was going on here that was beginning to intrigue me. What had my brother done? Whatever it was, I was beginning to think I might be able to turn the situation to my advantage. Because one thing was clear, this man was not here to court me. "Perhaps the two of you can tell me the reason for your visit now."

Kendrick moved further into the room. When I lowered onto the settee, he dropped into an armchair. Henry remained standing, hovering several feet away.

"Let me do the honors," Lord Kendrick said, watching me carefully, "since it is clear your brother lacks the courage to do so himself."

I was powerless to look away from the man's intense blue eyes, and my stomach did an alarming flip. There was something magnetic about him. An air that would draw every gaze to him.

I had never had such a reaction to a man's presence before, and heaven knows I'd been subjected to all manner of interactions during the season. But this man's amused, slightly mocking smile affected me more than the most ardent suitor.

He intrigued me. I would be alarmed if this had been anyone else, but everyone knew that the Legends weren't looking for brides. "Should I call for tea?" I said.

One corner of Kendrick's mouth lifted.

"That won't be necessary. I don't intend to stay long. But when your brother wasn't able to pay his gambling debt last night, he wrote me a promissory note."

I frowned at Henry. "That is most distressing, but I'm sure I don't need to be here for this interaction. Perhaps I should leave the two of you alone."

Kendrick's expression became decidedly less amused as he said, "But, my dear, this does concern you. Your brother, in lieu of payment, gave me his most precious family jewel. A diamond."

I frowned, turning over his words. Did we possess a diamond of such great value? It was possible, but I thought I knew about all the jewels in my mother's collection. I turned to look at Henry. "I don't understand. I was unaware that Mother possessed such a diamond."

He stiffened, then he motioned toward me with a wave of his hand. I caught his meaning immediately.

"Me? You wagered me?"

CHAPTER 3

KENDRICK

Steeling my nerves, I waited for the histrionics to begin. It was my least favorite aspect of dealing with the fairer sex. But instead, a heavy silence settled over the room. Brother and sister stared at one another, and I was surprised when Weston looked away.

Before I could break the silence, Miss Edwards spoke. "Perhaps you should leave us alone."

I assumed she was speaking to me, and I could understand why she'd want to berate her brother. At least she wouldn't make us all uncomfortable by doing so in my presence. But Weston's blustering protest made clear that rather than arguing with her brother, she wanted to speak to *me* alone.

Interesting.

"There's no betrothal," Weston sputtered. "I can't leave the two of you alone."

She stood, placed her hands on her hips, and stared down her brother. "Perhaps you should have thought of that before you *lost me* in a card game." She turned to look at me. "Do you have the promissory note?"

I tapped my coat where I had the note resting in an inside pocket. She nodded and turned to her brother with an expectant expression.

Giving up on convincing his sister, Weston turned to me. "I cannot allow this."

I rose to my feet and stared him down, the thought occurring to me that Miss Edwards and I were a matched set as we waited for her brother to fold.

He blanched. "But there is no marriage agreement."

I raised a brow. "Why on earth would you think I want to marry her?"

Weston turned to his sister, who lifted one shoulder in a casual shrug.

He turned then, his posture stooped with defeat, and left the room.

I shifted to face the curious Miss Edwards. She raised a hand and crossed to the drawing room door, where she proceeded to peek out into the hallway before closing it.

She didn't appear to be throwing a tantrum, so I braced for tears. But to my shock, she leaned against the door and laughed. "Oh, that was wonderful. Well done, my lord. The look on his face…" She burst into uncontrollable laughter.

My senses were on high alert now for another reason. "I hope that you and your brother don't expect me to marry you. If this is a ruse to force my hand because I've compromised you, you've miscalculated. Badly."

She fanned herself with her hand and took a few deep breaths, attempting to rein in her amusement. "No, no," she said between dwindling giggles. "Of course not." She actually shuddered then. "That is the last thing I want. Can you imagine what a disaster that would be, me expecting to coerce a Legend into marriage?"

I watched her carefully for telltale signs that she was lying but could see none. No fidgeting or faster breathing. And she had no difficulty meeting my gaze.

"Would you care to explain what is happening?"

Her laughter finally subsided, and she let out a soft sigh. I watched her return to the settee, then I settled into the armchair again and waited for her answer.

"I am only a month from my twentieth birthday."

That caught my attention. With her buxom figure, her blonde hair, and her undeniable beauty, I couldn't imagine how Caroline Edwards had managed to get this far without men doing everything in their power to secure her hand in marriage. Was it possible that she didn't possess a dowry?

In that case, I could well imagine those men making more inappropriate suggestions. Was that what Weston was doing here? Trying to find a wealthy protector for his sister? I wasn't immune to her charms, and if I'd met her at any other point, I would willingly take her to my bed. I might even set her up so I could enjoy her enticements at my leisure, despite the dramatic way in which my last such arrangement had ended.

But I wasn't here to debauch anyone's innocence, and it angered me that any man who pretended to be honorable would offer his sister up for such an arrangement.

"This is your third season?" The thought stretched credulity given that she was the diamond of the season. I refused to believe she'd been ignored for two seasons. What had Fairfax said about her? I'd been too angry to pay attention.

She shook her head. "No, it's my first season. My brother would have married me off two years ago if I'd allowed him. But I was just shy of eighteen, and I convinced Aunt Augusta that no harm would come of waiting a year." She sighed. "But since my birthday is in late June, that meant I was almost 19 last year."

"How did you manage not to have a season then?"

She shrugged. "It wasn't difficult to feign illness. A few coughs, a reddened nose from rubbing it. I even dampened my decolletage so it would appear as though I had a fever. Not wanting to occupy the same carriage, Henry was eager to leave me behind when he set off for London. Aunt Augusta was already in town, so when she discovered I wasn't with my brother…" She smiled. "It was already too late."

Against my better judgment, I could feel the

corners of my mouth stretching into a grin. "So you avoided the whole thing."

She smiled. "It was a glorious few months all to myself. My brother doesn't normally bother with me, but Aunt Augusta is very committed to finding me a husband. With the two of them away in London, I was able to turn away all the local suitors since it wouldn't have been seemly for me to entertain them alone."

I had to work to hold back a smile. "Of course not. So, what happened this year?"

"Aunt Augusta happened. She didn't trust Henry not to leave me behind this year, so she insisted we all travel together. I didn't try to feign illness this year. When she'd returned to Dorset last summer, she'd questioned the staff and learned I'd had a miraculous recovery after Henry's departure. This year, I could have been on death's door, and she would still have dragged me to London." She sighed. "I should have been more careful last year and pretended to be unwell longer. But I was so happy not to be in town doing all of this." She swept her hand between the two of us.

"So you finally had your debut, and you were named the diamond of the season."

She shuddered. "Yes, and it's as horrible as I feared."

"You don't wish to wed?" When she shook her head, I continued, "Do you prefer…"

She tilted her head, making clear she had no idea what I was asking.

"Are you drawn romantically to women?"

Her brow furrowed. "Is that a possibility?" She took a moment to think about it and finally shook her head. "I don't believe so, no."

"But you don't find yourself drawn to men."

She let out a soft huff, and I didn't miss the way her hands tightened in her lap. "Not before today, I didn't."

I couldn't deny that the compliment was a balm to my ego.

"It is most inconvenient since the two of us know that you are not in the market for a wife." She shook her head. "It matters not. In little more than a year, I will reach my age of majority. If I can keep my brother and aunt from forcing me to wed, I will be able to take possession of the money set aside for my dowry and gain my independence."

So she *did* have a dowry. I had to admit, I was intrigued by Caroline Edwards. Her levelheaded manner was a stark contrast to her brother's carelessness. I watched her closely as I returned to the reason for my visit. "There is still the matter of the money I am owed. I'm not in the habit of accepting women as payment for a debt."

"Yes, of course. I don't know what my brother was thinking."

She looked away, worrying her plump lower lip between her teeth. I was captivated by that small movement. With any other woman, I would have assumed it had been calculated to draw attention to her mouth. But my instincts told me she wasn't being coy, so I waited.

Finally, she straightened and met my gaze again. "What is the sum?"

I named it, and she winced. "I'll speak to my brother and see what can be done."

"And if he can't pay?" Promissory notes couldn't be enforced legally, but most gentlemen went out of their way to honor their debts. I didn't need the money, so I wouldn't go to the bother of calling him out. But that didn't mean I wouldn't let others know Weston couldn't be trusted to honor his obligations.

"In that instance, I'll pay the debt myself when I have the settlement from my dowry."

I balked at the suggestion that I was the type of

man to leave her destitute. "And then what happens to you?"

She smiled at my concern, as though she found me amusing. "My dowry is very generous. I should still have sufficient funds to set myself up modestly. I don't intend to live a lavish lifestyle. Don't worry on my account. I'll be fine."

Her confidence intrigued me. Just how large was her dowry? Added to her beauty, it was no wonder she'd been named the diamond of the season. She must be the target of every fortune hunter and ne'er-do-well. "And if you fall in love"—I forced myself not to sneer at the ridiculous sentiment—"and hand your dowry over to someone else?"

She laughed outright, and despite my better judgment, I found myself charmed by her sensible nature. "I've met every noble in town who is searching for a wife. You can rest assured I am in no danger of falling in love with any of them. I just have to keep Henry from coercing me into marrying."

I folded my arms across my chest and smiled. "He could try. But since I now own you until I'm otherwise recompensed, he won't be able to."

Her eyes widened, and her entire demeanor brightened. The effect was something to behold.

Fortunately, I'd been in the presence of many beautiful women and was mostly immune. Still, it was a pity I couldn't take her as a mistress. I had a feeling she'd be full of wonderful surprises.

"You are correct. He can't force me to marry when you possess his signed note saying I'm yours. You have the prior claim."

I raised a brow. "One that I won't be exercising."

"Of course not," she said, waving her hand in dismissal. "But no one needs to know that. Once word spreads about what happened, I'll be ruined."

I could detect a glint of devilry in her expression, which elicited an odd moment of panic. A fellow Legend had just fallen in love with—and married—the woman he'd been pretending to ruin. I forced my thoughts from that ridiculous notion. I was in no danger of falling in love with this woman in the way Moreland had fallen for his new bride. I'd need to marry one day, but that was still far in the future.

"What do you have in mind?" I asked. I half expected her to say she wanted to pretend to be my mistress, which I'd never let happen. I'd learned from Moreland's mistake.

"Nothing bad, of course. My aunt escorts me to

all the events around town." Her head tilted. "We're supposed to be attending the Henderson ball tomorrow evening." She blew out a breath. "I'm already dreading it. But once all my suitors learn that Henry has given me over to you…" She laughed. "Oh, this will be wonderful. Lord Penham will be enraged. I can't wait to see his expression."

I didn't have the heart to tell her that several men already suspected what her brother had done —certainly those who'd witnessed the card game at King's last night. They'd be watching to see whether their suspicions would be confirmed.

But the mention of Penham had me frowning. To say he was a nuisance would be paying him a compliment. "Has Penham been bothering you?"

She grimaced. "He's my brother's closest friend, and I've known him for most of my life. Of late, his attentions have been presumptuous, as though it is already decided that I'll marry him."

I managed not to swear aloud. "Has he forced his attentions on you?"

She shook her head, and I felt a measure of relief. "No, nothing like that. But between him and Henry, their insistence that I consider marrying Penham is beyond annoying."

The final piece of the puzzle I'd been trying to

decrypt clicked into place. "Penham has wanted you for some time, correct?"

Caroline's face twisted. "Unfortunately, yes."

"And has your brother always favored the match?"

She shrugged. "He didn't care. To be honest, I don't think he wanted to dwell on the fact that Penham had developed a romantic interest in me. But after our parents died and Henry came into his inheritance…" Her eyes narrowed. "He's been gambling a great deal lately."

I could almost see the way her mind was shifting through the recent series of events. She was putting the pieces together.

"Your brother wants the money set aside for your dowry," I said.

She was shaking her head. "But it would go to Penham if I married him, not to Henry."

I shrugged. "Given how sought after you are, it isn't difficult to believe that they'd come to an agreement on the matter. Your brother promotes the match and Penham agrees to give him a portion of your dowry after you're wed." I narrowed my eyes on her. "Just how large is your dowry?"

She shook her head. "I don't know, precisely. But I've caught Henry grumbling about the fact that he can't access the funds. Apparently, our father knew better than to trust him with it."

"Thank heavens for small mercies."

"Indeed." Her smile was sad, and I had to fight the urge to comfort her.

She continued, "So, if Henry needs me to marry Penham, why did he offer me as payment for his losses last night?"

I filled in the rest of what I'd deduced. "Because once word spreads that I've won you, you'll be ruined. People will assume that you and I…" When her cheeks pinkened, I chose not to voice the details. "Once you're ruined, no one else will want you."

"Except for Penham."

I nodded. "Yes."

She frowned. "I'm going to kill Henry."

I leaned forward, amused. "You won't gain your freedom if you're sent to the tower for killing your brother."

Her frown deepened, but then she sighed and met my gaze head on. "Will you help me?"

I smirked. "Much as I could see myself rising to the occasion of ending another's life, I'm afraid this situation doesn't merit that."

Her shoulders slumped. "That's fine. I don't

really want to see him die. But I am most vexed. I need to make him pay."

I was amused and, to my surprise, captivated by her intensity. I'd come here to return the promissory note currently in my pocket and force Weston to pay me. But now that I'd met his sister, I was curious to see how this situation would play out. "What do you have in mind?"

"Perhaps you could publicly stake your claim to me."

I smirked, and color flooded her cheeks.

"No, not like that. I thought perhaps you could attend a ball or two. Dance with me once, and the rumors will spread. I will become a social pariah." She grinned. "It will be wonderful."

"And then what? Your brother will think that his and Penham's scheme is working as planned."

"It doesn't matter. Since I'm not looking for a husband, I don't care if I'm ruined. I'll have my freedom that much sooner. Perhaps Aunt Augusta will allow me to stay home after that instead of attending the other events to which she's accepted invitations." She looked off into the distance, as though picturing it in her mind. "It will be delightful. I'll be able to stay home, with no more callers this season. And next year, when I reach my majority, I'll have control of my dowry."

"What if Penham decides to bundle you into a carriage and take you to Gretna Green?"

She frowned and looked at me. "Would he do that?"

I tilted my head and examined her. "I don't know. Would he?"

"I don't believe Henry would allow him to. Besides, as long as you don't renounce your claim on me…" She shook her head. "It would be unwise to cross a Legend, after all."

I could think of more than a few men who would love nothing better than to try, but they'd regret the attempt. The question was, did I want to be a pretend suitor? I narrowed my eyes. "I'm not going to marry you."

She folded her arms across her chest and leaned forward, mimicking my aloof disdain. "I wouldn't have you."

I grinned. Let the games begin.

CHAPTER 4

KENDRICK

The Mayfair Chronicle
Lady X

It seems the Legends are up to their old tricks again. Most recently, Lord K was rumored to be on the verge of marrying his mistress. But now he's moved on to loftier conquests. The on-dit has him courting the diamond of the season.

I swore as I dropped the broadsheet, which of course had Fairfax picking it up immediately to scan the article.

He chuckled. "You certainly have been a busy

boy. The rest of us are going to have to start picking up the slack. We can't have your antics taking up all the column space."

I pointed at him. "It's your fault that I'm in this situation."

Fairfax's smirk widened. "I told you not to take that bet."

I narrowed my eyes. "You're coming with me tonight."

"To speak to Weston?"

I shook my head. "I've already spoken to him."

Fairfax settled back in the armchair. "What did he say?"

"He didn't really have much to say. But I did meet his sister."

"The jewel that you won," Fairfax said with a nod.

I wanted to punch him but managed to restrain myself. "I don't know how Moreland puts up with you."

Fairfax grinned. "I am a constant source of delight. Now, help me to improve my game."

King's was busy this afternoon, but Fairfax stood and made his way to the one billiard table reserved for the Legends. With Moreland on his wedding trip, Fairfax was determined to make use of the time to better his game. Moreland routinely trounced him, and while Fairfax liked to pretend he wasn't bothered, he clearly was.

I watched as Fairfax lined up the balls in random order. Or it seemed like a random order, but as I watched him move through the motions of trying to pocket the balls, I realized he was replicating shots he'd missed during his most recent games. He still missed most of them now, but since Moreland would be gone for the next month at least, he had ample time to practice.

"So, where are we going?" Fairfax said as he reset the balls to run through the shots a second time.

I waited until he was just about to strike before saying, "The Henderson ball."

He missed, of course, and swore. "Are you out of your mind? I'm not going there. Would we even be welcome?"

The question was rhetorical, of course. We were welcome everywhere.

"If I'm going to be courting my diamond, you're going to be at my side."

Fairfax shook his head. "I still have two years before I turn 30. My mother has agreed not to press me about marrying until then, and I'm not going to frequent one of the primary marriage-mart events."

I smiled. "At least it's not Almack's. Yet."

Fairfax flung his billiard cue onto the table. "No, absolutely not. You're going to have to find someone else to accompany you to these events. Have you lost your senses? Now that Moreland is married, everyone's going to think we're all looking for brides if we're seen at the Henderson affair."

I shrugged. He was correct. If we showed up at the ball tonight, people would wonder whether we were planning to follow Moreland's example. But I'd be damned if I'd allow myself to be the sole object of that speculation.

Fairfax's eyes narrowed. "Please tell me you're not looking for a bride."

I laughed at the comical look of horror on his face. "Of course not."

Fairfax leaned against the billiard table. "Then why are we going to the Henderson ball?"

I smirked. "So you're coming with me?"

Fairfax scowled. "We both know you're going to force me, so I might as well come willingly."

He knew me well. But I wouldn't let myself feel guilty. I was in this situation because of him, after all. If I had to suffer, so did he. I recounted the conversation I'd had yesterday with Miss Edwards and explained her proposal.

Fairfax shook his head. "I don't know if this is wise. The last time one of us was asked to ruin a woman's reputation, he ended up marrying her."

It was impossible to forget that Moreland had married Rexford's sister. He'd been asked to ruin her in appearance only so that Rexford's father wouldn't force her to marry one of the worst men possible. But somewhere along the way, Moreland had developed feelings for her.

"That was an unusual situation. The two of them had to spend a great deal of time together under one roof. With all that heightened emotion and Moreland's sense of honor kicking in…" I shrugged. "She somehow slipped through his defenses. This situation is completely different. One, possibly two balls."

Fairfax shook his head. "If her dowry is as large as you say, do you really think that will be enough to keep the other suitors away?"

I shrugged. "There aren't many who would be foolish enough to cross us."

Fairfax narrowed his eyes again. "And if Weston comes up with the money he owes you? Would you give up your diamond?"

I met his gaze squarely. "As long as I have my money, they can have her."

Fairfax nodded. "Good. It's bad enough that one of us has fallen. We don't need to sacrifice anyone else to the marriage noose. We should see if any of the others want to come with us."

I frowned. "We don't need to make this a spectacle."

Fairfax grinned. "Of course we do. If you're going to put on a show for the ton, the rest of us should be given the opportunity to attend the performance."

"You're insufferable."

"Aren't we all?"

Fairfax headed toward the door, and I was forced to follow.

CHAPTER 5

CAROLINE

For the first time since arriving in London, I was excited to attend a ball. Thanks to either my brother's carelessness or his scheming, I would be taking my first step toward freedom tonight.

After dressing, I made my way downstairs. Henry was waiting for me in the drawing room. His scowl intensified when he saw I was dressed in a pale-blue ballgown that I knew made my eyes appear even bluer.

"You're not going to attend the ball tonight."

I gave him my most insincere smile. "Whyever not, brother dear?"

He was about to say something else, but Aunt Augusta chose that moment to enter the drawing room.

"Yes, Henry. Please tell us why the diamond of the season shouldn't be attending tonight's ball."

My smile turned triumphant as I watched Henry squirm. I added, "Is there something we should know?"

My brother's scowl deepened, then he turned and went to wait for us outside.

Auntie watched him go, a V forming between her brows. "What has gotten into him?"

I shrugged. "I have no idea."

She made a soft sound of displeasure. "I'm not sure why he cares since he'll probably spend the entire night in the card room."

I sincerely hoped that wasn't the case. He'd been doing more than enough gambling of late. Also, I wanted him to witness what was to unfold tonight.

Auntie and I followed Henry outside. My antici-pation was mixed with a healthy dose of doubt. Everything depended on whether Lord Kendrick kept his word.

When we'd spoken yesterday, he'd seemed agreeable to my suggestion that he attend the ball. But enough time had passed that he might have changed his mind. From all accounts, each of the Legendary Lords was wealthy. He didn't *need* the money my brother owed him, so he might have decided it wasn't worth the trouble to bother with me.

Henry was already waiting for us in the carriage, and he didn't bother to hide his glare when we joined him.

"What has gotten into you, nephew?" Auntie took out her fan and began using it with vigor. For early June, it was unseasonably warm. Auntie was going to be very uncomfortable in her high-necked gown.

The carriage began to move, and Henry leaned forward. "Penham has already made his intentions clear. If you'd allow him to court you—"

I raised a brow. "I wasn't aware that I was free to accept him."

His face paled as he darted a glance at our aunt.

Her eyes were narrowed on me. "Have you accepted someone's proposal without telling me?"

I smiled widely at her. "Of course not, Auntie."

"She means," Henry rushed to add, "that she intends to enjoy the rest of this season."

"Yes," I said with a small nod. "That is exactly what I meant."

And that wasn't a falsehood. If Kendrick didn't change his mind about helping me, I could very well see myself enjoying the rest of the season. With my name linked to that of a Legend, it would be a relief to see all the fortune hunters turn their attentions to someone else. I'd be able to spend my time chatting with the few friends I'd made this season.

The trip to the Henderson's large townhome was short, and before long, we were slowing. When the carriage halted, Henry exited first. As was his custom, he didn't turn to help us. He left that task to one of the footmen assisting with the carriages.

He seemed very anxious about how things would unfold tonight. Good. He should feel guilty after what he'd done—wagering me as though I were an inanimate object.

And if Lord Kendrick's assumptions were correct, my brother was trying to force me into a marriage he knew I didn't want. Thankfully, Aunt Augusta was my ally in this. Auntie made it clear that she wanted me to wed, but she was determined I choose my own husband.

The ballroom was already crowded when we were announced. Almost immediately, Henry made his excuses and headed for the card room.

Aunt Augusta watched him go with a small frown. "That boy. If he isn't careful, he'll bankrupt the estate."

I held back my wince. I didn't want to think about the fact that he might already be on the road to ruin.

I scanned the crowd, looking for friendly faces. I didn't see Lord Kendrick, but I did spot a friend. "Lady Diana and her family are already here." I started in their direction, and Aunt Augusta followed.

I'd taken a liking to Diana Atherton from the start. Early in the season, I'd seen her hovering around the edges of the room with her aunt and uncle, who I now knew were her legal guardians. Something about her open expression had called to me, and I'd made a point of befriending her.

Looking at her now, I couldn't understand why her aunt had dressed her in a yellow gown. Diana wasn't a fan of the color, and against her brown hair and hazel eyes, it brought out an unpleasant tone in Diana's pale skin.

I greeted Diana and her aunt and tucked my

arm through my friend's. I aimed my best smile at our respective aunts. "Would the two of you mind if I borrowed Diana? I'd like a refreshment before the dancing begins in earnest."

I could already see several men tracking my progress through the room and knew they'd soon be approaching to ask to sign my dance card. I made every effort not to make eye contact with any of them in what I knew would be a vain attempt to avoid the coming onslaught.

Diana's aunt waved us off, and I was relieved that Aunt Augusta chose to stay with the woman.

"Thank you," Diana whispered as we moved away. "I was quite tired of listening to my aunt's recital of my faults."

I shook my head. "Your only fault is succumbing to her insistence in dressing you in yellow. I think we're of a similar size, and I have a lavender gown that I know would look lovely on you. It would bring out the green in your eyes."

Diana sighed. "Aunt Matilda insists yellow is a lucky color. She says it will attract the attention of eligible gentlemen and make them think of sunny days." She fluffed her dress. "I don't know what is wrong with her eyesight when anyone can see that the color does not suit me. It makes me appear ill."

She glanced over my shoulder and sucked in her breath. She lowered her head quickly and shifted us to one side.

I barely resisted the urge to look over my shoulder. "Is something the matter?"

"Lord Clifton is here."

That piqued my interest. "Lord Clifton?"

She leaned in close. "He's one of the Legends."

My smile widened. If Lord Clifton was here, surely Kendrick would be as well. I refrained from turning to look for him. Lord Kendrick would find me soon enough. He was more adept at playing these games, after all. I was content to let him decide how tonight would proceed.

"Do you know him? How is it possible I'm only just learning that you have a connection with one of the Legends?"

She shook her head. "I don't know him well. My mother was friends with his mother."

I didn't press further. Diana's mother had died two years ago. My friend was 18 this year, which meant she would have been only 16 at the time. Her aunt and uncle had taken her in.

I was very curious about their acquaintance. "Do you think he remembers you?"

She shook her head. "I doubt it. I was still a girl

the last time I saw him. We were visiting his parents' estate, and I think he was home from school."

"It couldn't have been that long ago if you still remember him."

She shrugged. "Oh, look, Lord Fairfax is also here. Do you think we might be introduced tonight? He's very pretty."

She was changing the subject. *Interesting.*

"Is he?"

"He's standing by the garden doors. They call him 'The Fairest of Them All.'"

I couldn't help but laugh. The obvious play on his name was so unoriginal. "Perhaps Lord Clifton could introduce you to his friend."

She smiled, a hint of sadness in her eyes. "He wouldn't remember me."

I turned us so I could discreetly look over her shoulder. I spotted Lord Kendrick right away, and our eyes locked. He inclined his head in greeting then looked away. The saying was such a cliché, but I actually felt my heart leap. Next to him stood an equally tall man with fair hair. Lord Fairfax, no doubt. They were standing with a small group of men who were attracting a lot of attention.

I could hear the whispers grow in volume. "Legends," they were saying. "What are they doing here?"

I found it difficult to contain my glee. Lord Kendrick was proving to be a formidable ally.

CHAPTER 6

An hour later, my joy had dimmed. Beyond that single tilt of his head, Kendrick hadn't acknowledged my existence. Even worse, my dance card was now full, and I hadn't found a moment between sets to myself.

The only thing that made me feel better was that when gentlemen approached to claim a dance, many of them also claimed one with Diana. Her dance card wasn't full, but at least she wasn't spending the entire evening sitting with the wallflowers.

Aunt Augusta had joined a group of older

matrons and seemed content to spend the evening chatting with them. If I could manage to find a spare moment to myself, I planned to flee to the retiring room for a moment of peace.

If declining an invitation to dance wasn't considered so rude, I would have declined them all. Instead, I was passed from one dance partner to another, with scarcely a moment to breathe. I was just murmuring my thanks to my current dance partner, desperate to dip behind one of the large potted plants in the corner so I could snap one of the ribbons on my dancing slippers, when Lord Penham cut off my escape.

I let out a frustrated breath. Unfortunately, instead of keeping Henry company in the card room, Penham had been among the first to claim a spot on my dance card.

He dipped his head. "Miss Edwards, I believe this is my dance."

I held back my groan when the music for the next set began to play. Of course he'd managed to secure the first waltz for himself. My earlier happiness at seeing Kendrick was now eclipsed by my growing dread that he wasn't going to save me.

As though I'd conjured him, a figure approached to my right.

"My lady."

I turned, joy filling me at the sight of Kendrick standing there, quiet confidence radiating from him.

Penham frowned. "This is my dance, Kendrick."

Instead of replying, Kendrick simply stared at him. Then he raised a brow. Penham actually took a step backward, and I inwardly cheered.

When Kendrick turned back to me, I gladly took his arm and allowed him to lead me onto the dance floor. I barely managed to keep from laughing aloud when I turned back to see Penham staring after us, scowling. I took great comfort in having thwarted him but forced myself to look away. It wouldn't do to burst into peals of laughter.

Kendrick swept me into his arms, and we fell into the dance as though we'd been partners forever. I allowed myself to laugh freely then since anyone watching us would assume it was from delight.

I beamed up at my savior. "That was glorious. The look on his face when you simply stared at him. And the way he fell back when you raised a brow… Oh, to have such power." I sighed. "I wasn't sure Henry had told him what he'd done, but given the way he gave up so quickly, I think it's safe to assume he knows about the promissory note."

Kendrick's expression was neutral. "Penham is definitely aware of what transpired with your brother."

I shook my head and was careful to keep my voice low. "I still can't believe my brother thought he could force me to marry Penham by promising me to you. I've thought of little else in the past day, and it still makes no sense."

Kendrick tilted his head. "Why not?"

I smiled. "We both know you're not interested in me, but to hand your sister over to one of the Legends? He might as well have locked me in a bedroom with you."

When I saw a muscle tick in Kendrick's jaw, it occurred to me he might have taken my statement as a slight. "It's not that I don't think you're handsome. I'm sure any woman here would love to find themselves locked in a bedroom with you." I could feel heat coloring my cheeks. "Not me, of course. I'm not saying that I'd want to be locked in a bedroom with you…" I forced myself to stop rambling.

He laughed, the sound warm and deep. It did interesting things to my insides. "I must say, I didn't think I'd be this amused when you coerced me into attending this ball."

I frowned up at him, and he executed a series of turns that had me catching my breath as he swept us in and out among several dancing couples.

"You do this often," I said when he stopped showing off. "I shouldn't be surprised that one of the Legends is very skilled at waltzing. But no one has ever seen you at a ball."

He raised a brow. "No one? You've surveyed all of polite society?"

"Fine," I said with a sigh. "Perhaps I was exaggerating. I assumed that was the case since I don't follow your exploits. I've heard rumors of licentious behavior, but I don't know what that would entail. And I assumed that you wouldn't attend a ball since I hadn't seen any of you do so before tonight. I definitely would have noticed you."

He tugged me a little closer. "Trust me, my dear. If I'd been in the same ballroom as you before tonight, I know you would have noticed me."

A strange feeling unfurled somewhere within my heart, and I scowled at him. "Are you flirting with me?"

One corner of his mouth lifted. "I'm waltzing with you. Is it not part of the plan that I should be flirting with you as well?"

I thought about that for a moment and had to

concede he was correct. "Very well. I'm sure it will help matters if people see me enjoying myself in your company."

His grin widened at that. "I make it a point to always entertain the woman I'm with."

I couldn't help it. I laughed. He was so ridiculous. "At any rate, your duty to me will soon be over. I'm sure that after this waltz, I will be well and truly ruined."

He raised a brow. "Do you truly think that dancing with me once is sufficient to ruin you?"

I thought again for a moment. If he knew how to waltz, then he must have attended other balls. He'd danced with other women, and surely they hadn't all been ruined. "Perhaps a second dance then," I said with a nod. "We can search the other names on my dance card and decide which dance you can steal."

There was something in his expression that should have warned me about what he was planning.

"Are we being watched?" he asked.

He made a quick turn around the edge of the dance floor, and I glanced at the people who were watching. It might have been my imagination, but they *all* appeared to be staring at us. Even the other couples who were dancing. I hadn't noticed before now because I'd been so caught up in Kendrick's larger-than-life presence. But now I could see the way the couples closest to us seemed to be straining to overhear our conversation.

I met his gaze again. "I thought the attention I attracted before tonight was excessive, but the way everyone is scrutinizing you…" I shook my head. "How do you stand it?"

He lifted one shoulder, the movement slight but noticeable under my hand. "It can be useful."

Then before I realized what he intended to do, he danced me straight through the garden doors. The last sound I heard was the soft gasp of a matron who was staring at us, her mouth open in astonishment as we disappeared onto the balcony.

It took more effort than I thought possible not to burst into laughter at her outrage. I beamed up at him. "Well done, my lord."

CHAPTER 7

KENDRICK

I hadn't expected to be amused tonight. The last time I'd attended a ball was two years prior, and it had been a disaster. I hadn't been looking for a bride, but I'd thought it best to keep my eye on the marriage mart in case the perfect prospect appeared.

As it turned out, it was next to impossible to get to know anyone when mothers were ushering their daughters away from me. The only women who'd approached me that night were already married, which negated their candidacy as my future viscountess. After that evening, I'd vowed to wait several years before bothering with another attempt.

But tonight, as I looked down at Miss Edwards, it occurred to me that I was enjoying myself.

She smiled. "Well done, my lord."

I inclined my head. When she pulled her hand from my arm, I let her go, stifling the sense of loss I felt at her retreat.

Miss Caroline Edwards was beautiful, and I could understand why every man here clearly wanted her for himself. But I was used to being in the company of beautiful women. What had surprised me most tonight was how much I enjoyed her company. It was a shame we weren't meeting a few years from now, when I wasn't intent on enjoying the last few years of my bachelorhood.

She glanced over her shoulder then back at me. An older matron was peeking through the doors at us, but the woman retreated when my gaze met hers.

"Do you think this is enough to ruin me?"

She seemed genuinely gleeful at the prospect, and I couldn't help myself. "Perhaps. But if you want a guarantee, we should wander out into the gardens."

Caroline chewed on her lower lip, and my eyes

moved to her mouth. I couldn't help wondering whether she'd bite me if I tried to steal a kiss. But I'd never been one to force my attentions on an unwilling woman, so I waited for her response.

At her nod a few moments later, I held out an arm. She tucked her hand into my elbow, then we proceeded to the far end of the balcony and down the steps that led to the darkened gardens.

"I feel quite wicked," she said, her voice barely above a whisper.

I grinned. If she wanted wicked, I could certainly show her. "Is that an invitation?"

She laughed. "You are terrible. I can't believe my brother actually handed me over to you. What was he thinking?"

Weston was an idiot. He should be keeping his sister as far away from me as possible, not dangling such a tempting treat right in front of me. I said nothing as we continued our walk.

She leaned closer, and for a moment, I expected her to ask for a kiss. It shocked me how much I wanted that.

"I think…"

I held my breath and waited for her to continue.

She sighed. "I don't think my brother is very bright."

I chuckled. "That fact is not in dispute, Miss Edwards."

She nodded. "It is a good thing you and I are levelheaded about this situation."

I turned right and pulled her into a dark corner behind a large shrub. I looked down at her, and luminous blue eyes gazed up at me, tempting me beyond belief. "Would you call going out into the gardens, alone, with a known rake something a levelheaded person would do?"

She winced. "Normally, I'd agree that your point is valid. But in this instance, you and I have an agreement." When I didn't reply, she continued. "We both know this is temporary, that disappearing with you is a ruse to ruin me. After tonight, I'll need to ensure the scandal lasts through the next year. When I reach my majority, I'll have the money from my dowry to pay you what my brother owes you."

I wanted to tell her that I wouldn't accept money from her, but she didn't need to know that yet. For some reason, I didn't want to give her a reason to return to the ballroom. My motives were selfish, but she was also benefiting from our arrangement.

We both heard the footsteps at the same time.

Her eyes widened, a slight hint of panic in their depths.

"Someone is coming." She mouthed the words, and I managed to hold her back when she moved to peek around the shrub.

I lowered my head to whisper in her ear. "Are you sure you want to continue with this?"

She was frozen now, and I could almost see her practical mind warring with the fear of becoming the center of a scandal.

I continued. "If we're caught alone now, everyone will demand I marry you, and we both know that isn't going to happen."

We remained like that for what felt like an eternity, then she shook her head. It was the damnedest thing, but relief flooded through me. I didn't want to be the villain in her life story.

I drew her into my arms. When she wrapped her arms around me and rested her head on my chest, the urge to protect her was almost overwhelming.

The footsteps faded, and we waited another full minute before I reluctantly released her.

She wrapped her arms around her waist and looked away. "I feel like a coward. This was the perfect opportunity to make myself undesirable to all those would-be suitors, and I let it slip away from me."

I cupped her chin and tilted her face up to me. "It was never going to work, Caroline. Your brother would have seized the opportunity and continued to press you to marry Penham. At least now you still have the chance to find someone else."

The words felt bitter on my tongue, but they needed to be said.

She shook her head. "I don't want any of those men. But perhaps, since our association is at an end after this ball…"

My hand was still on her chin, and I couldn't resist running my thumb over her plump lower lip. "What would you like to ask me, Caroline?"

She shivered, and my pulse spiked.

"Would you kiss me?"

That was all the invitation I needed. Who was I to deny such a beautiful, intriguing woman?

CHAPTER 8

CAROLINE

This wouldn't be my first kiss. On two other occasions, potential suitors had wanted to prove their ardent admiration. Unfortunately, both attempts had been lackluster. After those unpleasant experiences, I'd made a point of turning my head when a suitor got too close.

But I couldn't help thinking that of any man I'd met, Kendrick would possess the skill my other suitors had lacked. A small voice warned that it wasn't wise to make this request of him. I pushed it aside.

When his mouth touched mine, a strange

feeling raced through me. I had no words to describe the sensation. I just wanted it to continue. His tongue stroked my bottom lip. I had a moment of doubt, but I trusted him and allowed him to enter.

I wasn't sure what happened next, but I knew I wanted to get closer to him. A yearning to press myself against him had me doing just that. He groaned into my mouth, then his hands began roaming up and down my back. One hand splayed between my shoulder blades, and the other cupped my backside, pressing me into him even more.

All the while, his mouth ravaged mine, and unexpected pleasure swept through my body. I rose up onto my toes, desperate to get even closer. I'd just touched my tongue to his, eliciting another groan from him, when I heard a shocked gasp.

Kendrick released me immediately, and it took me a moment to gather my wits. My only thought was that if I was ruined because of this kiss, I wouldn't regret it. I was glad I'd summoned the courage to make the request. When I turned to see who'd discovered us, I was surprised to find Diana standing there, her hands covering her mouth.

She rushed to my side and pulled me away from Kendrick. "I was about to turn back, telling myself it couldn't possibly be you making those noises. Have you taken leave of your senses, Caroline?"

Kendrick stepped back, and when I glanced at him, there was a gleam in his eye that told me he was amused.

I should have been grateful that Diana had interrupted us since one kiss from Kendrick caused me to forget where I was. The irony of the situation wasn't lost on me. I'd gone from wanting to be compromised to fearing someone might have seen us.

I looked past her. "Is anyone else out here?"

Diana shook her head. "No, of course not, although my aunt did see you come out here with Lord Kendrick. I told her that you'd asked me to meet you on the balcony after the waltz, and that Lord Kendrick was waiting with you until I arrived."

I felt a measure of relief. "Are you sure no one followed you out?"

"I didn't see anyone. But since it took me a few minutes to find you, I wouldn't be surprised if my aunt comes searching. I don't think she has the highest opinion of Lord Kendrick."

When I met Kendrick's gaze, he shrugged. "If

you change your mind, we can try again another time. Perhaps closer to the garden doors next time."

Diana thrust her hands onto her hips, her glare moving from Kendrick to me. "Have you lost your mind? Surely you don't want to be ruined."

I winced. "That was the plan originally, but then I lost my nerve. I thought that if I were ruined, no one would want me. The relentless attention would cease, and I'd be able to breathe again."

Diana laughed. "I don't think there's anything that could stop the others from wanting you."

I frowned. "Not even if I'm ruined by a Legend?"

She glanced at Kendrick. "He's not going to ruin you. I won't allow it."

Kendrick rocked back on his heels, but the gleam in his eyes was still there. "I don't believe we've been introduced."

I felt a hint of annoyance at the way he was watching Diana. Did he really think it necessary to flirt with her in front of me?

"This is Miss Diana Atherton," I said, turning to Kendrick. "She is newly out in society this year, and you are not allowed anywhere near her."

Kendrick met my gaze, one brow rising. "I appear to be near her now."

I let out an impatient huff. "Diana, this is Viscount Kendrick. And it seems you already know he is one of the Legends. We came out here so he could ruin me, but then I changed my mind."

Diana shook her head. "From what I saw, it didn't seem as though you'd changed your mind." She lowered her voice but not enough that Kendrick couldn't hear. "He won't marry you."

Remembering our kiss, I couldn't help but feel a pang of disappointment. But I forced myself to be practical. "No, of course not. I might have gotten carried away."

Diana made a sound that was between a laugh and a snort. "I'd say that's an understatement. At any rate, your plan was absurd. Lord Penham won't care if you're ruined. He's determined to have you."

I'd explained the situation to Diana, but I'd hoped Kendrick could find a way to help me. Her matter-of-fact statement had me feeling a touch of desperation.

Kendrick shrugged. "If what she says is true, we might have to tell everyone that I own you now."

Diana gasped. "What?"

I shook my head. "I'll explain it to you later." I turned to Kendrick. "Please don't tell anyone."

"Word is bound to get out," he said. "Your brother and I weren't alone at King's."

I winced. "Hopefully we can resolve this situation before Aunt Augusta learns about what happened."

Kendrick nodded in acknowledgement. "We can try it that way for now."

Diana was looking between the two of us then glanced back over her shoulder. "We need to return before anyone comes in search of us."

I sighed. "All right." I turned away from Kendrick, but then remembered something. "My slipper."

Kendrick glanced down. "Is something the matter with it?"

I glanced around, but when I didn't see a bench, I bent and untied the ribbons of one slipper. When I tugged on one ribbon and nothing happened, I let out a soft growl of frustration.

"Is something wrong with your ribbons?" From the tone of his voice, I could tell he was still amused.

I straightened. "I was hoping to rip one so that I would have an excuse not to dance for the rest of the evening. But my slippers appear to be disappointingly well made."

Kendrick was grinning now. He dropped into a crouch then looked up at me. "Would you allow me the honor?"

Heat flooded my face as I pointed my right toe and raised the hem of my dress several inches. My pulse began to race when he placed a hand around the back of my foot, his fingers curling against my skin above the slipper.

He was wearing gloves, and I was wearing stockings, but the heat of his touch seemed to burn through the layers of fabric. With his other hand, he took hold of one ribbon and yanked. The ribbon came clean off the slipper.

His fingers slid against the skin on the top of my foot before he rose to his feet again and handed me the ribbon. The gardens were dark, and I hoped he couldn't see my blush as I thanked him and took it from him.

"That should do," I said. "Now I won't have to dance again."

Diana slid her arm through mine, and we turned toward the house. When Kendrick fell into step with us, Diana drew to a halt. "Where do you think you're going?"

One corner of his mouth lifted. "I'm returning to the ball, of course."

"Not through the garden doors, you aren't." Diana tilted her head to the left. "I think there is a side door that way you can use. I'll return with Caroline. You can skulk in through the side door."

He grinned as he bowed his head. "As you wish." His gaze met mine again. "We will speak again on this matter."

I watched him turn and saunter off in the direction Diana had indicated. When he was gone from sight, Diana tugged on my arm, and together we made our way back to the ballroom. My smile widened as I allowed his parting words to wash over me.

He planned to see me again.

CHAPTER 9

REXFORD

I'd doubted the wisdom of attending this ball, but curiosity had won out. And the event would also give me the opportunity to deliver an important message.

My recent concerns about my sister had weighed heavily on my mind. Now that Victoria was married to Moreland and safe, the pair away on their wedding trip, my worry had eased. So when Fairfax had informed me of Kendrick's latest *acquisition* and that it had occurred in my club, I couldn't ignore the insolence.

It also wasn't outside the realm of possibility

that the situation might take an interesting turn. After all, one of our group had recently done the unthinkable and fallen in love.

I watched Kendrick approach the woman in question—Miss Caroline Edwards—who'd been declared the diamond of the season. Fairfax had assured me that Kendrick hadn't realized what was happening until it was too late and Weston had written his promissory note. But there had been witnesses, and I needed to make an example of the man. King's wasn't the type of establishment that disregarded the buying and selling of women.

When Kendrick and the diamond had escaped to the balcony, I turned to the other Legends and tilted my head toward the exit that led to the card room.

Fairfax, Greyson, and Clifton joined me as I went in search of my quarry. We were causing a stir, but that wasn't unusual when we were together. Speculation would be at an all-time high, and I couldn't help but wonder if our visit would be noted in the gossip column that liked to report on our activities. That was a situation I would need to deal with soon.

We entered the card room, which was exactly like every other one I'd visited. Oak-paneled walls, dark leather chairs, and mahogany tables laid out with packs of cards and ivory counters. The dark interior, heavy with the scent of tobacco smoke and brandy, was a stark contrast to the bright, gleaming ballroom.

I could understand why most of the men here had deposited their wives and daughters in the ball-room and escaped into this welcoming space.

I scanned the occupants of the room. Some of the younger men had been in the ballroom earlier. They'd danced, hurrying to claim their time with the most desirable of the young women newly on the marriage mart before heading into the card room.

But one man hadn't set foot in the ballroom after arriving with his sister. Baron Weston. The blighter who'd wagered his sister in my club.

A few aimed curious glances our way as we stood just inside the doorway, and I could tell by the way they tensed that they'd correctly interpreted my mood.

I strode to the table where, unsurprisingly, Weston was currently losing. His back was to us, but the other three at the table glanced up when we stopped.

I met each of their gazes and lifted my chin

slightly. Without question, they all turned over their cards and stood.

Weston let out a soft crow of delight. "I guess this is my lucky day," he said as he scooped up his winnings and dragged them to his own meager pile. The smile vanished when the four of us settled into the vacant seats.

I positioned myself directly opposite him, taking pleasure in the way the color drained from his face.

After a hard swallow, he straightened in a too-obvious attempt to hide his fear. "This is unexpected. I should probably leave you to it and see how my sister is doing, but I can indulge you in one hand." His eyes moved over us, then he stilled. "Is Kendrick not here tonight?"

I kept my gaze pinned on him. "He is otherwise occupied at the moment."

"Indeed," Greyson said. "I believe I saw him dancing."

Fairfax smiled. "I can't recall the last time I've seen him waltz."

Weston was growing increasingly agitated, especially as Fairfax continued, "But I don't believe he's waltzing at the moment."

"No." Clifton's tone was dry. "I believe he was

headed out into the gardens with a beautiful young woman. Who was that again?"

I kept my voice even as I said, "I believe it was the young woman he recently won in a card game."

Weston shot to his feet.

"Sit down," I said.

He stumbled back into his chair. "But my sister—"

I narrowed my eyes. "Yes, your sister, who you had the audacity to hand over as payment of a debt in my club. The club in which you are no longer welcome."

His mouth gaped open for a moment. "You should be the last person to criticize me, not after what happened to your own sister."

I leaned forward, my hand twitching on the card table. "Have a care about what you're going to say next."

Weston's mouth snapped closed.

Clifton glared at the man. "We don't peddle flesh at King's."

Weston shook his head. "That's not what happened."

"That is exactly what happened," Greyson said. "You handed your sister over as payment of a debt."

"He wasn't supposed to accept when he called the following day. I had it all planned out."

I leaned back and folded my arms over my chest. "You're not going to interfere with what happens next. Do you understand?"

"But she's my sister," Weston sputtered.

I'd rarely seen Fairfax angry, but he was angry now. "You should have thought of that before you wrote down her name."

Weston swallowed. "No one else read that note. No harm was done—"

"Everyone present knew exactly what you did," Fairfax said.

I'd had enough of this conversation. I stood, the others following suit. "You are no longer welcome at King's. Whatever happens now to your sister is on your head. Don't draw me into this again." I started to turn but stopped. "And you would do well to stay out of Kendrick's way."

The Legends joined me as I exited the card room, a silent wall of support I could always count on. I couldn't remember the last time I was so angry at someone who wasn't my father.

I had to force my hands to unclench. When we entered the ballroom again, I saw that two women were returning from the balcony. One was the woman who Kendrick now owned, and the other was a young woman I didn't recognize.

The two moved along the perimeter of the ballroom and made their way to the seating area set up for the ladies not currently dancing.

I made my way to the balcony, the others close behind. Kendrick stepped out of the shadows, and I strode to where he was waiting. "Have you accomplished what you came to do?"

Kendrick shrugged. "You go ahead. I'll join you at the club soon."

I wanted to give him the benefit of the doubt, but something about the entire situation had me convinced that tonight was only the beginning.

CHAPTER 10

KENDRICK

Rexford left, but the others chose to remain. They returned through the garden doors while I went in search of the side door Caroline's friend had assured me was here. When I found it, I easily made my way back to the ballroom.

I was content for now to leave Caroline to her own devices while I thought about the impulse that had urged me to drag her out onto the balcony in the first place. At that point, taking her into the gardens had been inevitable.

It wasn't the first time I'd disappeared into the

gardens with a woman, but I'd never done so with someone who was on the marriage mart and looking for a husband. Although I supposed that last statement didn't apply to Caroline either. She had assured me she didn't want to marry. At least not at this point in her life. But she would surely change her mind at some point.

That last thought shouldn't have bothered me as much as it did. Despite her brother giving her to me in payment of his gambling debt, she wasn't really mine.

I headed to the card room and was surprised Weston wasn't there. He'd been absent from the ballroom since my arrival. I couldn't help but wonder if he'd already run out of money and been asked to leave, but then another thought occurred to me.

When I returned to the ballroom, I found the other Legends standing off to one side. Sans Fairfax, of course, who was dancing. He wouldn't allow the opportunity to find a conquest for the night to pass him by.

But Greyson and Clifton were leaning against a wall, looking supremely bored. I suspected they were waiting for me to decide to leave. I scanned the guests and spotted Caroline off in the corner with the other young women who weren't dancing.

I smiled as I remembered the way she'd blushed when I'd touched her foot. She wouldn't be dancing again tonight, and the men who were hovering nearby were clearly unhappy to have missed their chance to try for the diamond of the season.

Caroline's aunt was chatting with a group of older women, and I spotted Weston off in another corner with Penham. My teeth ground together as I saw the way Penham was staring at Caroline. I forced myself to look away and headed to where Greyson and Clifton were standing, watching me.

"Did you enjoy yourself outside?" Clifton asked.

I shrugged. "It was interesting."

Greyson glanced to where Caroline was leaning over in her chair and laughing with Diana. "The two of them were here when we returned to the ballroom."

That confirmed what I suspected had happened while I was in the gardens. "You spoke to Weston?"

Clifton nodded. "Rexford wanted to tell him in person that his membership has been revoked."

I couldn't fault Rexford for that decision. "Weston is lucky that's all he did."

Greyson was watching Caroline's brother, his

eyes slightly narrowed. "For now, Rexford is content to monitor the situation. Time will tell if we'll need to take further action."

I could understand Rexford's annoyance with Weston, but that statement bothered me. It took me a moment to realize why. Rexford was acting as Caroline's protector, but she wasn't his to guard. She was mine.

I needed to tear up that promissory note, but I found myself reluctant to do so. For some reason, Miss Caroline Edwards intrigued me, and I couldn't recall the last time I'd been interested in a woman outside of what she could do for me in the bedroom.

Clifton was watching me again. "What are you going to do about the girl?"

I shrugged. "I haven't the faintest idea."

"Are you going to ruin her?"

My mind went back to the kiss we'd shared. I hadn't intended for it to get out of hand, but the moment I'd touched her, all my caution had fled. I couldn't help but wonder if Caroline would be interested in exploring more with me. She knew I wouldn't marry her, and she wasn't looking for a husband. There was nothing to stop us from having a little bit of fun.

My mood brightened considerably at the thought.

Greyson clapped me on the shoulder. "We're returning to the club. Are you joining us?"

My gaze drifted back to Caroline, and I couldn't deny that I was reluctant to leave. But I nodded at Greyson. Whatever was going to happen between Caroline and me would have to wait.

CHAPTER 11

CAROLINE

Thanks to Kendrick's assistance last night, I was able to avoid dancing with the remaining gentlemen who'd reserved a spot on my dance card. Unfortunately, they were not to be deterred, and I now found myself entertaining a steady stream of unwanted callers.

It was most vexing.

The only man I wouldn't mind seeing again was Lord Kendrick, but of course he wasn't here. I'd had a moment of weakness with him out in the gardens, but today I was determined not to think about the kiss we'd shared. His interest in me was fleeting. Honestly, given all of his conquests, I was flattered that he would bother with me at all. And there was something freeing about speaking to a handsome, eligible gentleman who had absolutely no interest in courting me.

Aunt Augusta had undertaken the daunting task of ushering the men out of our drawing room after their allocated fifteen minutes had passed. That was fourteen minutes too long for my liking, but I forced myself to smile and respond to repetitive observations about how nice the weather was today. At least their visits were of a relatively short duration, unlike Lord Penham's.

He'd arrived early and taken a seat by the front window. Because he was sitting with Henry, he wasn't technically calling on me, which meant Auntie couldn't ask him to leave.

He was acting as though he already owned me, and every time he spoke, which was far too often for my liking, I had to bite my tongue to keep from lashing out at him.

But midway through the afternoon, something interesting happened. Six callers were hovering in the drawing room when Lord Farrell mentioned

Lord Kendrick, at which point the Legend became all anyone wanted to talk about. Since the callers were overlapping, the gossip about his current activities continued. I couldn't stop myself from grinning as they spoke of him, which I knew would only increase speculation about his interest in me.

Each time the viscount's name came up, I glanced at my brother and Penham. Henry was displeased, but Penham was obviously annoyed, which brightened my mood considerably.

One caller—I couldn't remember his name—leaned forward and asked, "Is there any truth to the rumor that you and Lord Kendrick went out onto the balcony alone?"

Aunt Augusta stiffened. "Absolutely not."

I tilted my head to one side, affecting the air of someone who was confused by the question and ignoring the fact that he'd been unbearably rude to ask it in the first place. "Of course not. He merely escorted me out there so I could meet my friend, Miss Diana Atherton. We'd made arrangements to meet there after the waltz."

Since Diana and I had come in together afterward, the lie would be difficult to disprove. And I suspected that no one here had been aware of her whereabouts before that point. For all they knew, Diana had already been waiting for me.

Five men were speaking over one another in an attempt to get my attention when Auntie remarked that Lord Kendrick wasn't there.

As a new plan of attack occurred to me, I was powerless to keep myself from adding, "He mentioned that he had a very busy day today and gave me his regrets."

The young man who'd asked about him frowned. "Is he courting you?"

Aunt Augusta was quick to respond. "I don't think—"

"Yes."

Everyone froze, then an amazing thing happened. One by one, the gentlemen wished me a pleasant evening and took their leave. Happiness filled me when the door closed behind the last.

A few men were waiting outside, but when I walked over to the window, I could see the men who'd departed sharing what they'd learned. Again, one by one, each gentleman turned and left.

Aunt Augusta, who was standing next to me, turned and gave me a puzzled frown. "I don't think it's wise to encourage attention from one of the Legendary Lords."

"Henry has already spoken to Viscount Kendrick, and he's given him permission to court me." I smiled sweetly at my brother, who was starting to turn red.

"Is this true?" Aunt Augusta asked.

Henry looked at his friend before turning back to us. "I might have done something like that."

Auntie's brow furrowed. "Is that wise?"

I spoke before my brother could answer and ruin this for me. "Baron Moreland was married just last month. Which leads me to believe that the Legends might not be as irredeemable as people were led to believe." I turned to my brother. "I'm sure Henry would never have handed me over to Lord Kendrick without knowing the man's character."

Auntie's mouth dropped open in shock, and she whirled to face my brother. "Handed her over?"

"No, no." Henry was almost purple now. "She's trying to be witty. But I did let him know he could call on her."

"And I do so enjoy his company," I said, smiling sweetly at Penham.

When he rose and stormed from the room, I wanted to cheer.

My smile widened when the front door

slammed behind him. Apparently, I wouldn't need to be ruined after all. Simply being courted by a Legend would be enough to keep all the other unwanted suitors away.

I only hoped Kendrick wouldn't be too annoyed when he heard about my little fabrication.

CHAPTER 12

KENDRICK

I didn't enjoy attending proceedings in the House of Lords, but I took the task seriously. Especially when I could participate in a debate that would ruffle feathers. It wasn't a secret that the majority of those who attended every session did so because they wanted to ensure their way of life was preserved. They had little patience for considering reforms that might help people who weren't already blessed with wealth and position.

When tonight's interminable debate finally came to an end, I headed outside with Fairfax and Clifton. I envied Rexford and Greyson, who held courtesy titles and weren't expected to perform this particular duty.

"You seem out of sorts," Clifton said. "Does it have anything to do with last night's business?"

My thoughts immediately went to the kiss I'd shared with Caroline. I'd made a point of avoiding young women newly out in society, but I enjoyed her company a great deal. It surprised me that she didn't want a husband. I was sure she'd eventually change her mind, but I was content to help her for now.

And no one would fault me for wanting to thwart her brother's schemes. Really, I deserved a medal for my patience.

The situation wasn't at all similar to what had occurred with Moreland, who'd been asked to ruin Rexford's sister so she could avoid the marriage her father had arranged. They'd instead fallen in love and were now married and on their wedding trip.

Moreland's sudden change of heart was baffling. And if I were being honest, more than a little distressing. If I hadn't witnessed the entire series of events with my own eyes, I wouldn't have thought it possible. I understood desire, but almost from the moment he'd seen her, Moreland had become obsessed with Victoria. He'd tried to hide it, and I'd assumed it was just a physical attraction. Rexford's sister was beautiful, and no one blamed Moreland for desiring her.

I'd been shocked to learn he wanted to marry the girl and actually believed himself in love with her.

"I missed what happened," Fairfax said.

I shook my head. "You were intent on entertaining yourself elsewhere."

Fairfax smirked. "You brought me to a ball filled with beautiful women. I never realized there would be so many young widows."

"That's what happens when society seems intent on marrying their young daughters off to men who have one foot in the grave," Clifton said. His mother had been one such young woman, so I could understand the iciness behind his statement.

When we reached the carriages, Fairfax took his leave. I assumed he was returning to the bed of the woman with whom he'd left the ball.

Clifton and I made our way to where a groom was waiting with his curricle. We settled onto the leather seat, and I watched Clifton gather the reins and guide the matched pair of bays with practiced ease into the steady stream of vehicles departing parliament.

He glanced my way, a curious gleam in his eyes. "Are you planning to marry Miss Edwards? Or just make her your mistress?"

It took effort not to scowl. "Neither."

My last mistress had taught me that even *that* level of commitment was fraught with danger, as she'd leaked a story to *The Mayfair Chronicle* about me proposing marriage. I didn't know what had gotten into her, but the experience had taught me one thing. If Mirabelle's skill in the bedroom couldn't tempt me to marry, a proper young woman like Miss Edwards wouldn't accomplish that feat. And even though I had a note written in her brother's hand giving me possession of his sister, I wasn't foolish enough to think I could actually have her as my mistress. Society looked the other way when a widow took a lover, but they would condemn an unmarried young woman for doing the same thing, and I wouldn't do that to Caroline.

But as long as we were discreet, there was no reason I couldn't have her in my bed. If that kiss had shown me one thing, it was that Caroline possessed a passion I would enjoy exploring.

"Weston's sister is quite the beauty," Clifton said. "The others were more than a little annoyed last night to see you take an active interest in her."

I smirked, remembering the satisfaction I'd felt in stealing her for the waltz. "Penham is hoping to marry her, and Weston supports the match."

Clifton frowned. "He told you that after giving you his sister?"

I shook my head. "Miss Edwards did."

I could see him trying to work through that confusing bit of knowledge. It made no sense, after all, for Weston to give me his sister after losing a round of cards when he wanted her to marry another man.

"Her dowry is quite large, and Weston has been trying to get his hands on it."

Clifton grunted. "I'm not surprised he's finding himself constrained given his lack of skill at the card tables."

"Exactly. Caroline and I believe Penham has agreed to give her brother a portion of that dowry in exchange for promoting the match."

"That explains the way Penham was glaring at you last night while you waltzed with her. But it doesn't explain why Weston would write that note."

I couldn't hide my amusement as I recalled that first conversation I'd had with Caroline. "It seems that Weston is finding it difficult to convince his sister to fall in line with that plan."

Clifton grinned. "So she's smart as well as beautiful."

Clifton disliked Penham as much as I did. We'd known him during our years at Eaton. Instead of going on to Oxford, as we had, Penham had chosen to go on a grand tour. He'd never been particularly bright and had sneered at what he'd considered the uselessness of further education.

"She's told me she's not interested in securing a husband."

Clifton seemed to consider that statement, and I waited for him to come to the same conclusion Caroline and I had reached. It didn't take long. "Weston is hoping that if her association with you ruins her reputation, he'll be able to coerce her into accepting Penham." At my nod, Clifton continued. "And what is your involvement in all of this?"

I shrugged. "She's mine."

He shot me an amused glance. "Yours?"

"I don't expect that I'll be able to keep her. But if I help her to remain unmarried until she reaches her age of majority, the money set aside for her dowry will go to her. She's planning to set herself up somewhere and gain her independence. And she has assured me that she'll give me the money Weston owes me."

Clifton laughed outright. "She's the diamond of the season and has a large dowry. Does she honestly think she'll be able to escape marriage? She won't have to worry about you, but what's to stop someone else from attempting to compromise her? And then of course he'll offer to do the *honorable* thing and marry her. Frankly, I'm surprised Penham hasn't tried that already."

"While she belongs to me, no one will go near her." I didn't manage to keep my tone as casual as I'd hoped.

Of course, Clifton noticed. "You should have a care, lest you find yourself walking down the same wedding aisle as Moreland."

My intentions toward Caroline weren't that honorable. "You needn't fear that. I don't plan to marry for some time."

Clifton's gaze moved from the road to me. "Do you require our assistance in keeping the others away from her?"

I could tell that he didn't believe my assertion, but he was free to believe whatever he wanted. "I have it well in hand for now. And Miss Atherton proved to be very useful last night."

Clifton's brows drew together. "Miss Diana Atherton?"

I nodded, surprised. "Do you know her?"

"My mother was friends with her mother." I could see him searching his mind for a memory. When he found it, he said, "I believe Mother mentioned that Miss Atherton's mother died recently. Her father passed a few years ago. I believe she's now under the guardianship of her aunt and uncle."

I shrugged. I didn't really know anything about that. "Whatever the case, I went outside with Caroline, as you saw."

Clifton shook his head. "I don't know what you were thinking."

I hadn't been thinking. I hadn't been able to resist the temptation to get her alone.

"At any rate, Miss Atherton actually stormed out after us and dragged Caroline back to the ballroom. She even had the audacity to order me to return through a different door."

Clifton smiled. "She always was a bossy little thing. I can't believe she's old enough to be out in society. Are you certain it was her? I don't recall seeing her."

"She was easy to overlook. She was wearing a horrible yellow concoction that made her look like she was on death's door. If her aunt is trying to secure a match for her, she's doing a terrible job of presenting her in an alluring manner." I couldn't resist adding, "Do you have any interest in that direction?"

His mouth firmed into a line, his amusement at my expense vanishing. "When have I ever given you any indication that I was looking for a wife?"

I shrugged. "Moreland would have said the same thing a short time ago."

"No, I'm just thinking about the girl I used to know who was so full of life. Mother was quite fond of her. I think she'd hoped that the two of us would one day…" He shook his head. "Mother isn't holding her breath waiting for me to wed."

I barked out a laugh. "Mothers are forever making matches in their heads. For the most part, mine has remained silent on the subject of finding me a wife. I dread the day she decides it's time to press the issue."

Clifton lifted one shoulder. "I'm sure the girl is well taken care of. Her parents were well off, and I'm sure they made provisions for their only child. And heaven knows my mother is enough of a busybody that she would intercede if that wasn't the case. Now, about Miss Edwards. What are you planning next?"

I had no idea. I supposed I could attempt to learn where she was going to be tonight. Make sure that the vultures stayed away from her. And if Penham was also there, so much the better.

I was going to enjoy forcing him to watch as I took away his prize. I wasn't planning to keep her, but I could still have some fun along the way.

CHAPTER 13

CAROLINE

*L*ife would be so much easier if I didn't have to deal with Aunt Augusta's determination to secure a husband for me. Dealing with Henry was straightforward since he only thought about me when he was prodded to do so.

But I couldn't look at Auntie without remembering my mother, with whom she shared a striking resemblance. Auntie was going to be so disappointed when I reached the end of the season without accepting a marriage proposal.

Which was why I found myself at another event

tonight, but this time I hadn't uttered a word of protest. My performance last evening had caused Auntie a great deal of stress, and I felt the need to make up for it.

I consoled myself with the fact that I wouldn't have to dance tonight. We were attending a musicale being hosted to showcase the talents of Lord and Lady Farleigh's unmarried daughters. I was content to blend into the background and allow someone else to be the center of attention.

We'd been listening to the three Miss Farleighs sing and take turns at the pianoforte for an hour when Auntie leaned close and whispered, "Do you think they'll allow others to perform after the intermission?"

I gave her a small smile but said nothing. Simply sitting here, I was already attracting far too much attention. Lord Farleigh was burdened with three unmarried daughters, yet I could see the way several gentlemen kept glancing my way. I tried not to scowl at them for being unbearably rude.

So I paid attention to the young women's performances and clapped heartily at the end of each set. Fortunately, the three of them were very talented at the pianoforte, and their voices were quite lovely. They were just about to call for an intermission when I saw that Lord Penham had arrived at some point.

Unfortunately, I noticed him because he had the temerity to approach Lady Farleigh and whisper something in her ear. The woman's jaw tightened, her smile taut, but then she turned, her eyes scanning the crowd before landing on me. Dread settled in the pit of my stomach.

"I've been told that Miss Edwards is quite talented and that she loves to sing as well. I would consider it an honor if she'd join my daughters for one song."

I forced a smile, pushing back my annoyance, and rose to my feet. Auntie was clearly pleased with the turn of events, but I wanted to throttle Penham. His behavior was becoming increasingly problematic, and I knew he still expected to win my hand.

Ignoring him, I joined the three Miss Farleighs. I shifted so my back was to the audience and mouthed a silent "I am so sorry" to them. I then turned to the eldest Miss Farleigh, who was seated at the instrument, and watched her set up the music for a commonly known Irish air. She looked at me, and when I nodded my acceptance, she began to play.

My gaze swept over the occupants of the room.

Spotting Kendrick, I almost missed my cue to begin singing. He was leaning against the back wall, feet crossed at the ankles and arms folded over his chest. When our eyes met, he smiled, and my stomach turned over.

I tried to brush off the unexpected sensation and concentrate on not forgetting the lyrics to the song. I was surprised to see him here, and his presence meant I would enjoy the rest of the evening much more—for no reason other than I enjoyed his company.

I couldn't help but wonder if he was bored. Surely this wasn't the type of event he normally attended. Had he been here long? Even worse, had he witnessed Penham's horrible rudeness in forcing Lady Farleigh to invite me to perform when the first half was meant to showcase her daughters?

When the song was over, I dipped into a curtsy and turned to thank the three young women. They had much better voices than me, and I was relieved to finally escape the spotlight. My singing was passable, but no one would want to hear me perform a solo.

The guests were all beginning to stand now and heading in search of refreshments. Thankfully, Auntie reached me before Penham, who I could see heading our way out of the corner of my eye. I threaded my arm through hers and pulled her in the opposite direction.

"You don't seem happy," Auntie said when I found a small, unoccupied space to the left of the small stage.

"Penham was unbearably rude. It was clear to everyone that it wasn't time for guests to have a turn."

Auntie sighed. "He's made his interest in courting you clear. He's quite wealthy and is only a few years older than you. I don't know why you won't even consider him."

I almost frowned, but managed to stop myself in time. I didn't want anyone watching to think we were arguing.

When I didn't say anything, Auntie continued. "He can be insufferable at times, but so are most men. It would be a good match." She sighed. "Perhaps we should thank Lord Penham for thinking of you."

I'd rather ask him *not* to think of me, but I couldn't say that out loud.

"Imagine my surprise at finding the two loveliest women in all of London here tonight."

Kendrick's words settled over me, and I smiled.

For the first time tonight, I didn't have to feign delight at a gentleman's compliment.

"Lord Kendrick," I said, turning to greet him. "You flatter us."

Auntie's eyes narrowed slightly as she watched him. "I didn't take you for the type of man to attend musicales."

A corner of his mouth lifted. "I am a man of many interests." His gaze slid to mine on the last word, and anyone observing would think that he was referring to me.

I found myself wanting to believe him. He offered me his arm, and I took it. "There is no dancing tonight, my lord."

"No, but there are refreshments." He turned to my aunt. "Your niece and I will bring you a cup."

Of course he wasn't the kind of man to ask for permission. He was informing Auntie he wanted to speak to me in private. I could see the momentary indecision in my aunt's eyes, but the room was crowded, so nothing untoward would happen. Auntie inclined her head, and I could feel her gaze on us as we walked away.

I lowered my voice. "What are you doing here? Despite your statement to the contrary, I imagine this is the first musicale you've ever attended."

He smiled. "It is, but I was recently informed that I'm courting you. And if that's true, I thought it best if all the other gentlemen who are even now watching you and trying to figure out how to pry you away from me realize that I have a prior claim."

I winced. "I didn't expect word to reach you so soon. But in my defense, it's surprising that anyone would be foolish enough to believe your motivations would be that honorable. And you're not one to care about what others say about you."

His eyes lit with amusement. "It appears you know me far too well."

"Your reputation precedes you. So, why are you here?"

He leaned down, moving his head closer to mine. Anyone watching would think he was murmuring compliments in my ear.

"Is Penham being a nuisance?"

I sighed. "He is the bane of my existence. I can't believe he was so rude as to coerce Lady Farleigh into inviting me to sing."

"I saw you sitting off to one side, attempting to appear invisible. Is that normal behavior for someone who's sought after by every gentleman?"

"You know how much I hate all the attention I

attract. For once, I was content, as others were center stage."

Kendrick tsked. "Have no fear. I'll sit with you for the second half of the performance and ensure Penham stays away."

CHAPTER 14

KENDRICK

Grim satisfaction twisted through me when I caught Penham's glare from across the room. With the aim of sinking my blade deeper and causing the man the utmost annoyance, I leaned even closer and murmured in her ear. "Penham is glaring daggers at us."

She laughed and smiled up at me. This close, it would be so easy to kiss her again.

"You are terrible. I wouldn't be surprised if he calls you out."

I tried to picture it. "He can try, but I doubt he'd find any satisfaction in the act."

A surprising number of people were in attendance, and they were all heading toward the refreshment tables set up along one wall, so our progress was slow.

"What should we talk about now?" Caroline said. "Should I laugh again? Pretend that you are the most entertaining gentleman in the room?"

I frowned with mock distress. "You wound me. I'm sure you don't need to pretend to enjoy my company."

Caroline pressed her lips together, but she was unable to hide the merriment in her eyes. "I think your ego is already far too large, my lord."

Now I had to hold back *my* amusement. "Does that mean you're not happy to see me?"

Caroline smiled again, one of her genuine smiles that lit her eyes and made her even more beautiful. "On the contrary, I am delighted. Aunt Augusta was about to force me to thank Penham for thinking of me, after which he would have surely tried to monopolize my attention for the rest of the evening."

I could imagine the scene all too clearly. "He's always been annoying and has always assumed everyone is delighted to be in his company."

Caroline seemed surprised. "You know him well?"

I shrugged. "We were in school together for far too many years. Let's just say we've never been on the friendliest of terms."

I saw no point in shocking her with some of the antics bored youths could get up to. And Penham had been squarely in the camp of those who'd wanted to take down Rexford and his friends. Because of that history, I'd never ignored an opportunity to one-up the man. Even now, the feel of his eyes on us had me tugging Caroline closer to my side.

Of course, I made sure to step closer to another couple so the maneuver would appear casual, as though I was merely trying to ensure she wouldn't bump into them. But the amusement on Caroline's face told me she knew exactly what I was doing.

When we finally reached the refreshment table, I released Caroline and performed the honors. Ratafia, of course. I handed one glass to Caroline and poured a second glass for her aunt.

She tilted her head. "None for you?"

Throwing caution to the wind, I poured a third glass. Hoping it wouldn't be as sweet as some liked to make it, I saluted her and raised the cup to my lips. I took a small sip.

Interestingly, I tasted more than the customary hint of brandy. I had no doubt Lady Farleigh had been behind that decision. She was probably hoping the added spirits would induce gentlemen to view her daughters more favorably.

When I met Caroline's gaze, her eyes were fixed on my mouth. A familiar heat began to stir within me.

"If you keep looking at me that way, I'm going to take it as an invitation that you want me to kiss you again."

She cleared her throat and glanced away. "The horror. I can't imagine why anyone would want to do that."

Our gazes met and held for a long moment, and I knew she was remembering the kiss we'd shared. She hadn't been horrified then.

I made a silent vow to show this woman that she was wrong if she thought all men were cut from the same cloth. If Penham was the type of man she was attracting, I could understand why she didn't want to get married. But that left the door open for men like me, who would be more than happy to show her there was life beyond the staid respectability of marriage or spinsterhood. A third choice I had no doubt she'd find more enjoyable.

Someone cleared their throat behind us, and I realized we were blocking access to the refreshment table. I murmured an apology and led Caroline away. I was carrying two glasses and couldn't offer her my arm, but she stayed close to me. When we reached her aunt, Lady Fredricks accepted her glass with a circumspect thank you. She then proceeded to drain half her glass without batting an eye.

Clearly, she wasn't as surprised as I'd been by the liberal amount of spirits in the refreshment.

I watched Caroline and her aunt discuss the performance. I'd arrived just before the last song and had seen Penham approach Lady Farleigh to make his request. After witnessing his clumsy attempt to gain Caroline and Lady Fredricks's gratitude, I took a great deal of delight in stepping in and frustrating his plans.

The intermission was over all too soon, and footmen were circulating among the guests to collect the empty cups. I handed over mine, which was still half full. Even generously laced with brandy, ratafia was still far too sweet for me. But Caroline and her aunt had both drained their cups.

I murmured a request to a footman, and he

brought an extra chair so I could sit next to Caroline and her aunt. Unfortunately, Lady Fredricks made sure to take the seat between me and her niece. Caroline met my gaze behind her aunt's back and murmured an apology. I winked by way of reply. If Caroline's aunt thought I could be so easily thwarted, she'd soon realize just how wrong she was.

The rest of the evening passed by quickly enough. For the second half, several other guests were invited onto the small platform to showcase their talents. When Lady Farleigh glanced our way, Caroline shook her head. Lady Farleigh nodded and moved on to another young woman.

Lady Fredricks tried to hide her displeasure, but she leaned in to whisper something to her niece.

Caroline raised a hand to her throat. "The air is so dry in here. It's a miracle I managed that first song. Perhaps I'm coming down with a cold."

Her eyes met mine before darting away. She was lying. I set aside that little piece of information. Caroline couldn't maintain eye contact when she wasn't being honest.

Lady Fredricks pursed her lips in annoyance. She didn't press the issue, but she definitely didn't believe her niece's excuse.

When the musical part of the evening was over, Lady Fredricks took her charge firmly in hand. "Since you're not feeling well, we should get you home. We wouldn't want you to miss the Hatfield Ball tomorrow night."

Caroline sighed. "Of course not, Auntie." She turned to me and dipped into a curtsy. "It was a pleasure seeing you tonight, my lord. Perhaps we shall see each other again soon."

Why was I entertaining this nonsense? Despite my better judgment, I dipped my head in a small bow. "I think that can be arranged."

Lady Fredricks said her goodbyes to the hosts and whisked her niece away.

I turned to look at Penham. He made no attempt to hide his glare. Had he been scowling this whole time?

I smiled at him, enjoying the way his frown deepened, and turned to leave.

I hadn't accomplished anything that evening, but I now possessed an important piece of information. Caroline was going to be at the Hatfield Ball tomorrow night. I was already looking forward to getting her alone again.

CHAPTER 15

CAROLINE

*E*very eligible young woman in town for the season now wanted to be my close and personal friend. The unending parade of gentlemen callers had disappeared and was now replaced by callers of the fairer sex. It started when Diana paid me a visit shortly after midday. We saw each other often, so I wasn't surprised to see her.

Then the Miss Farleighs arrived. Their appearance was more surprising. After last night's musicale, I would have expected them to stay home, waiting to see if any young gentlemen would call to pay their respects. Then one by one, a stream of other debutantes began to arrive.

And they didn't just stay for the few minutes dictated by polite society. Instead, they made themselves comfortable in the drawing room, occupying every available space, and started chatting amongst themselves.

Normally, most of these young women tried to avoid me. I'd heard one of them say that standing next to me made their own beauty shine less brightly. Apparently, they had no such reservations when it came to visiting me privately today.

I wasn't surprised when they started talking about the Legendary Lords. "Baron Moreland married Victoria Wright last month," the eldest Miss Farleigh said. "When the season started, Mama warned us that the Legends weren't interested in finding brides and that we shouldn't entertain any attention they paid us."

I bit back my comment that it was unlikely any of those men would be actively searching for a bride amongst young women just entering into society. Yes, it was true that Viscount Kendrick was paying me a surprising amount of attention, but they didn't know the real reason behind his actions, and I wasn't about to explain it to them.

Diana leaned forward in her seat next to me on the settee. "Victoria is the sister of the Marquess of Rexford. She must have known Baron Moreland for some time, so it's not surprising that they wed."

One of the others who normally shunned me—I couldn't for the life of me remember her name—lowered her voice to the most outrageous of stage whispers and said, "I heard he ruined her first, and then he married her."

Their voices were now a cacophony of speculation as another jumped in to add, "Do you think Rexford forced the baron to marry his sister?"

Diana shook her head. "I heard it was a love match and that anyone who sees the way he dotes on her wouldn't believe he was forced into the match."

I leaned back against the settee and crossed my arms. "Whatever the case, we must remember that Moreland wouldn't ruin Rexford's sister. They're close friends, and from all accounts, they would never betray another Legend."

The youngest Miss Farleigh, who was just in her first season, smiled shyly at me. "What can you tell us about Viscount Kendrick? People can't decide whether he's courting you or trying to have his way with you."

I couldn't help laughing. "If I allowed the viscount to take any liberties with me, there would be nothing to stop him from just walking away afterward." I tried not to think about the kiss we'd shared. "Do you really think it would be possible to force one of the Legends into marrying?"

Diana frowned as she jumped to my defense. "Do the lot of you think Caroline is that foolish? She would never allow him to take such liberties."

She carefully avoided looking at me when she spoke since the two of us knew I *was* that foolish. If not for Diana and her intervention out in the gardens, I might be ruined right now.

I didn't miss the way the others smiled slyly at one another, and I knew exactly what they were thinking. In their minds, the fact that I had blonde hair and blue eyes and was praised for my beauty all but branded me as also being empty-headed. Diana was the only one amongst them who'd befriended me, and she knew that wasn't the case. It was bad enough when men assumed I was young and foolish. I hated that other women believed that as well.

They were still whispering and talking over each other, wondering which of the other Legends might start paying attention to them. It hadn't gone unnoticed that the other Legends had attended the

Henderson Ball. I glanced at Diana, wondering if she would offer any information about the Earl of Clifton, but she was staring down at her hands.

Someone mentioned that Viscount Fairfax had been the only other Legend to dance that evening. Several eyes lit up at that news, but the eldest Miss Farleigh crushed their hopes when she pointed out that he'd only danced with widows.

Some of the women were so innocent they obviously didn't know the significance of that statement, but when Diana glanced at me, I could tell she wasn't one of them. Fairfax wasn't looking for a bride. He was spending time with women who would be happy to warm his bed.

"Why do you think Kendrick is courting you?"

I didn't catch who'd asked the question, but the middle Miss Farleigh made a small sound of disgust in response. "She's the diamond. Who wouldn't want her? Frankly, he's doing the rest of us a favor. Now that he's made his interest clear, the other men might start paying attention to the rest of us."

There were murmurs of assent and agreement.

Henry chose that moment to enter the drawing room. He paused in the doorway, pretending to be surprised to see so many young women present. But I knew my brother far too well. One of the footman would have told him what was happening, and he'd decided to come down and see for himself. He loved being the center of attention, and aside from Diana, the women gave him exactly what he wanted. It was nauseating the way they vied for his attention, sitting up straighter and tilting their bodies so as to put their bosoms on display.

The eldest Miss Fairleigh, who was sitting near the door, dropped her handkerchief and tittered when Henry bent down to retrieve it for her.

Diana leaned closer and whispered, "Should we tell them that he has no money?"

I shushed her. "Aunt Augusta would murder us."

She sighed. "We'll just have to make do with taking notes and mocking them once they leave."

I smiled at her. What would I do without my closest friend?

CHAPTER 16

CAROLINE

Near midnight, I began to accept that Kendrick wouldn't make an appearance at the ball tonight. I'd spent the first hour inundated with requests from gentlemen who wanted to sign my dance card. When the music began, I spent the rest of the evening dancing with many of the same gentlemen who'd been trying to capture my interest all season.

I'd spent much of the night looking around the ballroom, hoping to spot Kendrick's familiar form leaning against a wall, a small, sardonic smile on his lips. More than once, I'd dragged my attention back to my dance partner to find that he'd asked a question I hadn't caught. Fortunately, little was required of me beyond a smile and a murmur of assent or noncommittal gesture. Men weren't interested in me for lively conversation and were content with that interaction.

Kendrick was the only man who'd ever gone out of his way to engage me in conversation. Distracted yet again by thoughts of him, my gaze wandered to the garden doors. I couldn't seem to stop thinking about when he'd led me outside into the gardens.

A few gentlemen had commented on the beautiful evening and how delightful the gardens must look under the full moon. Instead of replying, I'd simply widened my eyes, pretending to be shocked that they'd make such a suggestion. The look was enough to send them into a stammering attempt to change the subject.

No one else would be leading me outside. The last thing I wanted was to be married to one of these men. When it was time for the waltz, I straightened and forced myself not to cringe as Lord Penham approached. Kendrick wouldn't be saving me from this unwanted waltz tonight.

I dipped into a curtsy when he stopped before me and gave him a polite smile that was far from genuine. Every other gentleman with whom I'd danced had been content with that, but Penham was always insufferable. From his smug smile, it was clear he thought he'd scored a win.

I suppose he was handsome enough with his light-brown hair and pale-green eyes, but he wasn't nearly as attractive as Viscount Kendrick. And I'd known him far too many years to be fooled by his attempts to woo me.

When he escorted me to the center of the dance floor, I tried not to frown as I thought of how much I'd enjoyed waltzing with Kendrick. Penham wanted to ensure everyone would see me on his arm. I was used to his attempts to appear more important than he was, so I ignored it. And thankfully, when the music started, he didn't try to draw me closer than what would be considered respectable.

I suppose I had his friendship with my brother to thank for that because he was exactly the sort of man to try to take liberties. Our prominent positioning also ensured everyone would notice if he behaved in such an improper manner. And if there was one thing important to Penham, it was his reputation. He thrived on everyone thinking he was honorable, which was laughable given that he was scheming with my brother to trap me into marrying him.

He tried to engage me in conversation, and I brought out my usual half smiles and noncommittal murmurs. With each one, his frown deepened. Finally, he leaned close while executing a turn—one not nearly as skillful as Kendrick's—and whispered into my ear, "I don't know what game you're playing with Kendrick, but he'll only disappoint you."

When he moved back to a respectable distance, I met his gaze and laughed. For the first time, he'd said something that amused me.

"Do you honestly believe I'm foolish enough to think Lord Kendrick has any romantic interest in me?"

He was careful to keep his face neutral when he replied. "I've seen the way he looks at you."

I laughed again. "I'm sure it's not any different from the way every other man looks at me."

A slight frown marred his careful expression before he smoothed his forehead again. "You're courting disaster. Men like Kendrick are too dangerous for the likes of you."

Penham had succeeded in accomplishing the one thing no other man had managed to do that evening. He'd brought out my true emotions. I'd been feeling increasingly detached as the hours passed, but at his words, a spark of anger ignited within me. How dare he act as though he had my best interests at heart?

He only cared about my dowry and winning me as a trophy to show off to all the unsuccessful suitors. A slight shudder went through me as I wondered what it would be like to endure a kiss from this man, to share the marriage bed… I forced my thoughts away from that image and glared at Penham.

If his haughty expression was any indication, he thought he had the upper hand. "You should be afraid, Caroline. It would be best if you ceased all association with the man."

I tilted my head and somehow managed a tight smile. "That would be exceedingly difficult given what my brother has done. Viscount Kendrick has more rights to my attention than any other man, including you."

Penham's jaw tightened. "What does that mean?"

I shook my head. "You should speak to my brother. It appears he's holding back a few details."

Thankfully, the waltz came to an end then.

Penham bowed, and I dipped into a curtsy. But I could no longer look at his smug, self-satisfied smile.

"I will call on you tomorrow."

I lifted one shoulder. "So will every other man I danced with tonight. You can do as you wish, but you should know that nothing will come of it."

He escorted me back to my aunt, and I counted myself fortunate when he said nothing further. This was the last dance for me tonight, and I couldn't wait to leave. The ball would continue for a few hours yet, but Auntie didn't enjoy staying out very late.

Diana intercepted us before we reached my aunt. She looked up at Lord Penham and dipped into a deep curtsy before turning to smile at me. "I know you are planning to leave soon. Can I steal you away for a few minutes?"

"Of course." I took her arm, relieved to be done with Penham. But I could feel his gaze on us as we left the ballroom.

"The retiring room is down this hallway," Diana said.

I frowned. "I thought it was to the left."

Diana shook her head. "You are very much mistaken. We want to go this way."

I knew I was correct, but something in her expression caused me to nod and follow her.

We passed a darkened room with the door ajar, and I felt goosebumps form on my arms. I opened my mouth to tell her we needed to return to the ballroom when an arm reached out and pulled me into the room. A hand covered my mouth, muffling my cry of surprise.

Diana's expression was serious as she looked past me to my assailant. "You have exactly five minutes. I'm going to the retiring room and will be back soon."

To my shock, she closed the door and left me there.

"You're safe, Caroline."

The soft words spoken in a familiar voice, coupled with the welcome scent of sandalwood, sent a shiver of awareness through me. I sagged with relief. When he released me, I turned to face him.

Kendrick stood there, looking wickedly hand-some in the darkened library. If he were any other man, I'd be frightened right now, but I knew he would never hurt me.

I wanted to smile. Heaven knew I was happy to

see him. Instead, I placed my hands on my hips and forced myself to glare at him. "You frightened me."

He smirked. The expression wasn't too different from the way Penham had looked at me, but for some reason, it didn't grate on me when Kendrick did it.

Heat burned in his eyes as he looked at me. "We certainly can't have you screaming in alarm."

CHAPTER 17

KENDRICK

I stared down at Caroline, hands planted on her slim-but-shapely hips, her mouth compressed into a thin line of annoyance that I knew she didn't feel. I couldn't stop thinking of all the more pleasurable ways I could make her scream.

"You didn't save me," she said.

I raised a brow. "Were you in danger?"

She huffed and dropped her hands to clasp them more sedately at her waist. "Only of being bored all evening. I was also subjected to the annoyance of having to waltz with Lord Penham."

One corner of my mouth lifted in amusement. It still amazed me that this woman, who was sought after by every eligible bachelor looking for a bride, hated that she could have her pick of any man.

"A waltz," I said with a small hum. "I seem to recall you enjoying that particular dance."

"You know very well that I was referring to the partner I was forced to endure."

I rocked back on my heels. "So you admit that you enjoyed waltzing with me."

She made a valiant effort to hide her amusement before giving up and laughing. "You know very well that I did, but that is because I know you don't want to marry me."

"Perhaps there are other things I would like to do with you." I watched her reaction carefully, but she either didn't believe me or she didn't want to.

"You don't need to tease me. We both know that you have no interest in me. Now tell me, is there a reason you're hiding in the library? We could have had this discussion on the dance floor."

"And deprive you of waltzing with Penham?"

This time, her annoyance was genuine. And I don't know what it said about me, but I enjoyed seeing it. It seemed I appreciated contrary young women who didn't go out of their way to fawn over me to get my attention. Caroline's straightforward nature was a breath of fresh air.

I shrugged. "I wanted to see you, but I didn't want to go through the ordeal of hanging around the ballroom and pretending I don't see the speculative glances aimed my way."

Caroline sighed. "It's quite annoying, is it not? People watching everything you're doing, trying to decide if you're giving preferential treatment to one person over another. I wouldn't be surprised to learn they're placing bets on who I'll marry."

I almost didn't have the heart to tell her. "What would you say if you learned that Penham was the current favorite?"

The way her face crumpled in distaste had me smiling.

"I'd say that he's whispering in certain people's ears and telling them his acquaintance with my brother means that there's been a long-established understanding."

This woman never failed to surprise me. She was far more intelligent than any of those men out there gave her credit for. She'd discerned exactly why Penham was the favorite.

"Tell me, my lord," she said, taking a step closer. "What are people saying about our acquaintance?"

I took a corresponding step toward her. "People are wondering if I'm going to ruin you."

"That is most distressing," she said with exaggerated shock.

I laughed. I'm not sure how I managed it, but I refrained from pulling her into my arms and doing just that.

She looked up at me, one brow raised. "Was there a reason you needed to speak to me in private?"

I shrugged. "No reason. I just wanted to see how you were doing."

I'd surprised her. Frankly, I'd also surprised myself, but it was the truth. For some reason, I cared about this young woman. I told myself it was because she was technically mine until her brother's debt was settled, but I knew that wasn't entirely true. It didn't matter, however, because nothing serious could happen between Caroline and me.

She took a final step closer and placed a hand on my arm. When her tongue darted out over her bottom lip, a thrill of anticipation surged through me. And in that moment, all my assumptions about her scruples were thrown out the window. Caroline wasn't looking for a husband, but that didn't mean she wouldn't consider another type of arrangement.

Even in the darkened room, I could see the desire in her eyes as she watched me.

"Tell me, my lord…"

When she hesitated, I lowered my face to hers, which was now tilted in the universal signal that she wanted me to kiss her. "Yes, Caroline."

She licked her lips again and I wanted to groan. "I was thinking about the way I reacted when you kissed me the other night."

When she didn't continue, I realized she expected me to leap at the unspoken invitation. But if Caroline wanted to do this with me, I needed to know that it was something she wouldn't regret.

"And?"

Her eyes narrowed, and for a moment, I thought she was going to pull away. Instead, she rose up on her toes. "Could you kiss me again?"

She didn't need to ask twice. My mouth was on hers, my hands reaching up to cup her face, when the door to the hallway opened slowly.

"Oh, good heavens," a woman said in annoyance. "You promised me that you weren't going to try to debauch her."

I let out a frustrated breath and raised my head to look at Miss Diana Atherton.

Caroline let out a corresponding sigh. She

turned to look at Diana and shrugged. "You can't really blame me."

Diana shook her head. "Are the two of you finished? I peeked into the ballroom and saw your aunt looking for you."

Caroline glanced back at me, and I could see her reluctance to leave.

"Go ahead," I said. "I'll see you tomorrow."

I watched her turn and leave. When the door closed behind the two young women, I found myself staring at the space where she'd been standing. I couldn't hold back my grin. Miss Caroline Edwards was turning out to be a delightful surprise.

CHAPTER 18

CAROLINE

The most aggravating part of a London season was having to devote so much time pretending to enjoy the company of the large number of people wanting to speak to you. The burden was that much worse when you'd been named the diamond of the season.

I glanced over to the corner of the drawing room where Auntie was smiling out the window at all the men streaming through the front doors in a seemingly unending parade. I could only imagine they'd noticed Kendrick's absence at the Hatfield ball last night. They probably assumed he'd grown tired of me already. I couldn't blame them since I knew he wasn't actually courting me.

My cheeks were beginning to hurt from smiling so much. Fortunately, because so many gentlemen were calling, I only had to speak to each one for a few minutes before they had to take their leave.

As he had the other day after the Henderson ball, Penham arrived early and was sitting next to my brother. Even though I tried to ignore him, I could feel his self-centered air of superiority radiating from him. I wanted to ask the butler to escort him out, but my brother was head of this household. And since neither he nor Auntie seemed bothered by Penham's presence, he was an immovable obstacle in my life.

I glanced at the clock over the mantel and was relieved to see that it was almost four o'clock. Calling hours were almost over. The last visitor had just left, and my duty was over for the day.

To my annoyance, Penham rose and joined me on the settee. He sat far too close and ignored the scowl I aimed at him.

"Miss Edwards," he said. "Caroline."

I narrowed my eyes but didn't say anything.

"Now that everyone has gone, I think you and I should speak privately."

I looked over at Henry, who was smiling widely. I imagined how satisfying it would be to stand up, walk over to where he was sitting, and kick him. Had he encouraged this nonsense after what he'd already done with Kendrick?

"Perhaps we can put this off until I'm feeling better. I didn't sleep well last night and entertaining all these callers has tired me."

He lowered his voice so only I could hear him. "You can't ignore me forever."

I planned to do exactly that. I was about to stand and excuse myself but stopped when I heard another knock at the front door. I wanted to groan. This afternoon was never going to end.

Then I heard Lord Kendrick's voice. I smiled and congratulated myself for informing the butler that I was always home for Lord Kendrick. Penham leaned back, his arms folded across his chest. His smirk faded when we heard the butler allow Kendrick into the house.

The Legend stopped in the drawing room doorway and took in the scene. My mood instantly improved. Last night I'd accused him of not coming to my rescue. Today he'd more than made up for that because he'd just saved me from Lord Penham's uncomfortable attention.

I rose to my feet. "You are late, my lord, but our house is always open to you."

He smiled at me. Then I saw the flowers he held. Every other man had brought roses. Red roses, white roses, a few had even thought to distinguish themselves by bringing yellow roses. But Lord Kendrick had brought lilies.

I crossed over to him and accepted them. I buried my face in the bouquet and inhaled the scent.

I looked up at him. "How did you know that lilies are my favorite?"

His eyes met mine. His voice was low when he said, "I pay attention."

I frowned. "I'm fairly certain I've never mentioned it."

"At the Henderson ball, before we danced, I watched you. Whenever you passed by an arrangement with lilies, you reached out to touch them. You did the same thing last night."

He was right—I did do that. I shouldn't have been surprised that he'd noticed. "I didn't think you were there last night."

He shrugged. "I was in the ballroom briefly. Then I saw Miss Atherton and enlisted her assistance."

I raised a brow. "So you could have saved me earlier."

One corner of his mouth quirked. "You seemed to be doing fine on your own."

We looked at each other for what seemed like a very long time before my brother spoke.

"What brings you here, Kendrick?"

He turned to face Henry. "I'm just keeping an eye out for what is mine."

Aunt Augusta gasped, and I felt as though I was going to faint. I touched Kendrick's arm to get his attention.

"She doesn't know," I whispered.

Kendrick met my gaze and nodded. He leaned close and spoke in my ear. "I won't offer the information, but I won't lie if asked."

I swallowed thickly and nodded. Lord Kendrick had nothing to hide, after all. Henry was the one who'd acted badly.

Aunt Augusta stood and crossed over to us. I stared at her, clutching the bouquet of lilies to my chest.

When she stopped in front of Kendrick, she said, "I think we need to have a conversation, my lord."

He raised a brow. "Now?"

"No. Alone." She turned and looked at Lord Penham and Henry. "The two of you need to go somewhere and do something else right now. I have to speak to Lord Kendrick." She turned to look at me. "You, too, Caroline. I'll speak to you later."

Alarm spread through me, and I turned to Kendrick.

He nodded. "All will be well."

I turned to Auntie, hoping she couldn't see the panic threatening to swamp me. "If you need to speak to me, I'll be in the music room."

At her tight smile, I turned and quickly left the drawing room. The last thing I needed was for Penham and Henry to follow me.

CHAPTER 19

KENDRICK

Caroline's concern had been written plainly on her face before she turned to leave. I hadn't lied when I'd assured her that all would be well. At some point during our short acquaintance, I'd grown to admire her, and I would do everything in my power to save her from distress.

I watched as Penham and Weston left the room. I wanted to see if they'd try to corner Caroline. Their voices were low when they reached the hallway, and I couldn't make out what they were saying. After a brief conversation, Penham turned toward the front door, and relief flooded through me when I heard the door close behind him.

I turned to face Lady Fredricks, who was watching me. Looking at her, I had the impression that Caroline would look very much like her aunt when she reached a similar age. Unless I was mistaken, Lady Fredricks was in her late forties and still a very attractive woman. A smattering of silver hair threaded through the blond at her temples, and her figure was still slim and elegant. She was a widow, but that was all I knew about her.

Her gaze never wavered. "What are your intentions toward my niece?"

Well, now I knew something else about her. She was as straightforward as Caroline. I didn't think I'd be able to get out of this conversation without revealing the truth, but I owed it to Caroline to at least try.

"Your niece is a beautiful young woman who is also intelligent and in possession of a sharp wit. I enjoy spending time with her."

Her eyes widened when I mentioned Caroline's intelligence, and I knew why. Most men who looked at her wouldn't see anything of her mind. They were only concerned about what lay on the surface.

"Does that mean you're interested in courting

her? Because if that's not the case, I need to ask you to step aside. People are talking. They've noticed your interest in my niece, and I fear the speculation might jeopardize her chance to find a husband."

Caroline didn't want a husband, but it wasn't my place to make that announcement. And it certainly wouldn't paint my interest in Caroline in the best light if I revealed what I knew.

"Your niece and I have become friends."

From the look on her face, it was clear she didn't believe me. I wouldn't have believed it possible myself a few short days ago.

Lady Fredricks straightened to her full height. "So what you're telling me is you're not looking for a wife."

I silently apologized to Caroline as I nodded. "You are correct in that assumption."

She clasped her hands at her waist and nodded. "Very well. Then you should leave, and I am asking you to stay away from my niece. The next time you see her, act as though you are not acquaintances."

"I'm afraid I can't do that, my lady."

She drew back as though I'd struck her, but she rallied quickly. I could see she was about to insist, so I did the one thing that would end this argument. I reached into the inner pocket of my coat and pulled out the promissory note her nephew had penned.

I gave it to her and watched as she unfolded it and read the scrawled lines. Her eyes widened, and I noticed a slight tremor of her lips before she pressed them together. She refolded the note and handed it back to me.

"Tell me that note isn't real. That this is some sort of jest you are trying to play on my niece. I know that the Legends have a certain reputation, but I never thought—"

"Do you know your nephew's handwriting? Because I don't. I'd never seen it before he wrote that note."

She closed her eyes, and I watched as she took a deep breath before facing me again. "This cannot be happening. Please tell me he didn't write you that promissory note."

I tucked it back into my pocket. A promissory note was an odd thing for me to be carrying around at all times—but no stranger than someone giving me their sister as payment for a debt. Carrying the note close to my heart had absolutely nothing to do with my protectiveness toward the young woman.

"I would never perpetrate such a forgery. You have my word on that."

She stared at me for several long moments.

When it was clear she didn't know how to proceed, I offered the only suggestion possible. "I think that you need to take this matter up with your nephew."

She took another deep breath and nodded. The determination I'd seen in her was now replaced by fatigue. Her entire body sagged, and I couldn't help but feel a hint of guilt, which was damned annoying. I wasn't the one who'd set us all on this course. I was simply trying my best to help Caroline through what could have been a horrible situation. I didn't want to imagine Weston signing a marriage contract between her and Penham without her consent.

Caroline was a determined young woman, but she cared about her family. Weston could conceivably convince her the marriage was her duty to the family.

"I can assure you I'll do just that," she said.

"I'll take my leave then." I didn't want to, but I knew when to make a strategic retreat. Lady Fredricks needed to speak to her nephew right now.

I turned to depart but stopped when she spoke again.

"You should be aware, my lord, that I am very

protective of my family, and I am not done with you. We will speak about this again."

I dipped my head. "I would expect nothing less."

I could definitely see where Caroline got her spirit.

CHAPTER 20

CAROLINE

In a vain attempt to distract myself from worrying about what was happening between Auntie and Lord Kendrick, I tapped away at the keys of the pianoforte. I tried to play a song but couldn't concentrate on the music.

What was he telling her? I'd felt the need to keep Henry's actions secret from Auntie, but Kendrick wouldn't lie to protect my brother. How upset would she be when she learned the truth?

I didn't have to wait long before Auntie entered the room. "We need to talk."

With a deep breath, I folded my hands in my

lap and turned on the bench to face her. I looked past her, but of course Kendrick wasn't there. She would have asked him to leave after their conversation.

Auntie's stiff posture and the tight line of her jaw telegraphed her anger. I swallowed and stood. "About what, Auntie?"

She frowned. "Where is your brother?"

I closed my eyes briefly. Auntie *did* know, and there would be no avoiding her anger. Even worse was the knowledge that we'd disappointed her.

"He's in his study."

Hopefully without Lord Penham.

Aunt Augusta nodded and swept from the room. I hesitated, fighting the urge to flee. But Auntie had come to see me first, and that meant she expected me to follow her. She could have asked one of the servants where Henry was, but she'd said she wanted to talk to me as well.

I hurried after her and had just caught up when she stormed into Henry's study.

My brother was seated at the desk, a frown of concentration on his face that turned into surprise as he looked up. Unless I was mistaken, he was examining the accounting books. He should have paid them more attention *before* he decided to gamble away all of his disposable income. I tried not to think about how much he'd lost.

"I'm busy, perhaps we can speak later——"

"As you know," Auntie said, "I've spoken to Viscount Kendrick. He shared some very distressing news with me."

Henry rose to his feet. "You can't believe anything he says."

Auntie placed her hands on her hips and glared at him. I've been on the receiving end of those glares, and I was glad it was aimed at someone else right now.

"He showed me the promissory note, Henry. It was written in your hand."

My brother stilled, and I could tell he was trying to come up with a convincing lie. But when he realized there was no way to avoid the truth, his posture deflated.

"I can't believe you were so reckless. What could have possessed you to do such a thing?"

"It will work out——"

"You gave your sister away to settle a gambling debt! And to one of the Legendary Lords!"

Henry stiffened, and from his mutinous expression, I could tell he was going to try to bluster his way out of this. I folded my arms across my chest and waited to see what he would say.

"What I did was no different from what men do when they arrange marriages for their siblings or their daughters. All this nonsense about allowing a woman to choose—"

"She is your sister! And there is a great deal of difference between arranging an advantageous match for her and giving her to a known rogue to settle a gambling debt."

Ignoring the slight against Kendrick, I turned to my brother. "Henry knows better than to arrange a marriage without my consent. He wouldn't want the embarrassment of watching me refuse to say the wedding vows when prompted by the vicar."

Henry pointed at me. "This is all your fault. If you'd just choose someone, we could all get on with our lives." He turned to Auntie. "Kendrick is trying to get a rise out of me. He's angry that I bested him—"

I laughed. "If you had to give him a promissory note, then it sounds like he's the one who bested you."

Henry ignored me. "I have the matter well in hand. You don't need to worry."

Auntie was holding herself dangerously still. "I

was tasked with introducing your sister to society. I promised your mother on her deathbed that I would ensure Caroline was taken care of. I thought she was being overly protective by insisting I oversee the task, that surely she'd be able to trust her son to take care of his sister. But it seems your mother knew you'd bungle everything."

The color drained from Henry's face, and I decided it was best to change the subject from our mother. "What exactly did Viscount Kendrick say?"

Auntie turned to face me. "Given the fact that everyone is talking about the unexpected attention he's been showing you, I asked him about his intentions."

My heart began beating faster, but I told myself it had nothing to do with Kendrick. I was simply concerned about the worry we'd caused Auntie. But I couldn't seem to stop myself from asking, "What did he say?"

The pity in my aunt's eyes was unmistakable. "He's not looking for a bride."

Auntie's words shouldn't have bothered me. Kendrick and I had already discussed this, so I wasn't suffering from any illusions that he'd fall madly in love and want to marry me.

"Of course not. He's a Legend, after all. Why

would he be interested in marrying when he could have any number of women in his bed?"

Auntie's mouth dropped open then snapped closed. "Please tell me you haven't been one of those women."

I wanted to scream at myself for my outburst. Somehow this conversation had turned from Henry's wrongdoing to my own *innocent* actions. "Of course not. When have you known me to have my head turned by false flattery?"

Although I was fairly certain that Kendrick's flattery hadn't been false. Or had it?

Auntie turned back to Henry. "What are you going to do about this?"

Henry's hands were fisted at his sides. "I have a plan."

I scoffed. "Excuse me for not trusting you." He winced at the word *trust*, which I'd used deliberately to remind him that our mother hadn't trusted him either. "You handed me over to another man without speaking to me first. And it wasn't even a marriage agreement. I am not a toy to be passed around amongst your friends and acquaintances at your whim."

Henry's face was now red, and I know that our

aunt's presence was the only reason he wasn't yelling at me now.

Auntie glanced between the two of us. Finally, after a tense silence that seemed to stretch forever, she flung her hands up. "What are we going to do? People are whispering. And when there's no marriage announcement at the end of the season, Caroline will be ruined."

I hesitated but then let out a long breath. I was going to have to give away my plans. "I still have my dowry."

Henry came around the desk. "Absolutely not. You can't be foolish enough to think he'll marry you."

I turned to snap at him. "You gave me to him. You have no say in what happens between the two of us now."

Auntie placed a hand on my arm. "Perhaps we can leave London for the rest of the season. Kendrick won't follow."

I shook my head. "There's no need. I've spoken to Lord Kendrick on this matter and we've reached an agreement." I saw the way Henry's jaw tightened, but he wisely chose to remain silent. "When I reach my age of majority, the dowry becomes mine.

I have told Lord Kendrick that I will give him the money Henry owes him from those funds."

Henry paced away then turned to face me again. "That money—"

"Is mine. It is supposed to go to my husband. And if I don't marry, it will come to me."

Auntie was watching my brother with a frown. Her gaze went to the open account books on his desk and back to him. "What have you done, Henry? Please tell me you have the money to settle your debts. Then your sister will be free from the man's attention."

Henry dropped into his chair. When he didn't reply, Auntie reached for the account books.

Henry slammed the volume closed. "I have matters well in hand. I need to make a few arrangements first, then I'll speak to Kendrick and clear up this whole mess."

Auntie sighed. "You'd better hurry before your sister's reputation is ruined."

Henry snorted. "She'll be fine. Everyone wants her. And Penham—"

"I am *never* going to marry Penham," I said, refusing to let him finish that sentence.

I turned and stormed from the room. But I

couldn't help worrying about what my brother was going to do now.

CHAPTER 21

KENDRICK

*D*eciding it would be best to stay away
from Caroline for the rest of the day, I
didn't even try to discover where she'd be tonight.
Instead, I made my way to King's. It was late afternoon, and the club would be filling with those who
wanted to avoid the social events of the season—the
bachelors not yet ready to settle down and the older
gentlemen who made a point of ignoring their
wives.

Penham would probably turn into one of those
husbands.

I pushed away the annoying thought. Caroline

was smart enough to evade whatever trap the man tried to concoct with her brother. They'd erred when Weston chose to involve me. Just because I wasn't looking for a wife didn't mean I would allow them to force a bright light like Caroline to marry against her will.

When I reached the club, I made my way to the billiard room. Fairfax was bent over one of the tables, continuing his quest to improve.

"Who's put that scowl on your face?" The question hadn't come from Fairfax.

Surely I was mistaken… I turned to face the gentleman with the deep voice and was shocked to see Moreland.

"I thought you were on your wedding trip. Certainly you haven't grown bored of your wife already?"

A slow grin spread across his face. "Never. To my shock, I find that marriage suits me. Who could have imagined?"

I clapped him on the shoulder and laughed, following him to a free billiard table. "Did you get tired of separating Fairfax from his money?"

"I'm feeling generous today and letting him practice for a bit first."

He set up the balls and allowed me to take the

first shot. We all knew he was the best at billiards, but occasionally one of us could win a game. Except for Fairfax, of course. He played abysmally.

"I'm surprised you returned to town so soon. I didn't expect to see you again until after the end of the season."

Moreland waited until my turn was over before replying. As good as he was at the game, he didn't need to resort to distraction while his opponents were taking aim.

He took his first shot and straightened to face me. "How could I stay away when I heard you'd won the diamond of the season in a card game?"

I swore and closed the space between us. Thankfully, he'd kept his voice low. There were several men in the room who couldn't be trusted with that information.

My own voice was barely above a whisper. "Who told you that?"

He put down his cue stick and faced me, one brow raised. "Did I hear incorrectly?"

"It was Fairfax, wasn't it? I'm going to wring his neck. Did he also tell you that he suspected what was happening and didn't warn me?"

Moreland leaned back against the table and folded his arms across his chest. "I heard he wanted to warn you, but you insisted that you knew what you were doing."

"Well, clearly, I didn't." I would never admit aloud that when I considered all the men with whom Weston could have set his scheme in motion, I was glad he'd chosen me. Many would have tried to force Caroline into their beds that first night.

Moreland was watching me carefully, and I waited. He definitely had something to say about the situation. He wouldn't have cut short his wedding trip just to laugh at my expense.

Finally, he shook his head. "It was Rexford."

That surprised me. Rexford wasn't one to gossip. He was, however, known for strategic maneuvering. "Why?"

Moreland shrugged. "Perhaps he thought I could give you advice on wooing a proper lady."

I scowled. "If I didn't know Rexford would kill me for causing his sister any distress, I'd call you out for that."

Moreland grinned. "He just wanted to let me know in case you needed our help."

"I'm not wooing—"

Moreland shook his head, his smile widening. Honestly, why was he so happy? It was disconcerting. "Victoria is acquainted with Miss Edwards.

Rexford thought it might be prudent to have his sister in London in case she needs to intercede."

I didn't like the sound of that. "In what way?"

Moreland shrugged again. "I have no idea. But when Victoria heard the news, she was eager to return in case Miss Edwards needed her support. Apparently, she believes you're going to break the woman's heart."

"Well, she needn't concern herself. Caroline isn't looking for a husband. She just wants my help in keeping the others away."

Moreland straightened and picked up the billiard cue again. I watched him as he made quick work of the remaining balls on the table, thankful we hadn't placed a wager on this game.

"What are you going to do about the money Weston still owes you?"

I explained the scheme Caroline had outlined for when her unclaimed dowry came into her possession. I probably should have called a meeting of the Legends and explained it to everyone in one go.

"So it seems you have the entire matter well in hand," Moreland said with a nod.

"For now. But Penham is determined to have her, and he's close to Weston. They're hoping that

I'll ruin her reputation and discard her, and then he'll step in and claim her for himself."

Moreland winced. "Penham was always more style than substance. I certainly don't envy her having to suffer his attention." His eyes were fixed on me when he continued. "You could always let him have her."

"No."

Now it was Moreland's turn to clap me on the shoulder. "Careful, old man. You sound a tad possessive there."

"I've given her my word. Besides, it's not as though I'm desperate for the blunt. When the time comes, I'm not going to accept her money."

"You could if you married her."

I shook my head. "Even if I wanted to…" I frowned when I saw the way his face lit up. "I'm *not* saying I want to marry her. Just that in the unlikely event I took leave of my senses, like you did, she wouldn't have me. She's not interested in marrying."

There was a knowing smirk on Moreland's lips that had me longing to join him the next time he entered the boxing ring. "So you're just tolerating her company?"

I leaned back against the billiard table. "I'm

passing the time. Besides, it's vastly entertaining watching Penham tie himself up in knots when he sees me anywhere near her."

"Are you going to ask her to be your mistress?"

I ignored the way my body lit up at that thought. It was vastly annoying that I'd very much like to do that. But Caroline would never agree, and I didn't actually want to ruin her. That would be playing right into Penham and Weston's hands.

"I won't be making that mistake again. Not after what happened with my last mistress."

Moreland nodded in sympathy. He'd been here at the start of the season when Mirabelle had spread rumors about me asking her to be my wife.

"But you *would* bed her."

I shrugged. "I'm human. Of course I would if the opportunity presented itself." And I dearly hoped it would.

Moreland clapped me on the shoulder again. "Victoria and I will be here if you, or Miss Edwards, need us. Now, I need to see Fairfax. He won a sizable amount of money from me at cards the last time I was here. I need to even up the score."

I watched him join Fairfax and Clifton at their billiard table. Fairfax winced and cursed Moreland.

With a sigh, I decided to join them. Their antics would help distract me from thoughts of Caroline. I had no doubt Lady Fredricks had already spoken to her and Weston. I just hoped Caroline's aunt wouldn't make things difficult for me, because I had no intention of staying away from her niece.

CHAPTER 22

CAROLINE

$\mathscr{I}$ was shocked when Aunt Augusta didn't insist we go to the theater tonight as originally planned. She'd never paid any attention to my musings about how nice it would be to have a quiet evening at home, insisting we needed to be seen at every event.

Her sudden change of heart caused me no small amount of concern. After the argument in Henry's study hours ago, I didn't see her again. The staff told me she was feeling under the weather and had asked for her dinner tray to be sent up to her room. Since Henry was out, I'd also eaten alone in my room.

I should have been taking this opportunity to bask in the silence, perhaps spend the evening reading , or… I frowned.

The hours stretched out before me, and I didn't know how I was going to pass the time. I couldn't very well write to my acquaintances back home since everyone with whom I would normally correspond was in London for the season. Perhaps tonight would be a good time to start a diary.

It was nine in the evening, and I was essentially home alone. How ironic that for the first time this season, I didn't want to be home. I wanted to go out and, hopefully, run into Lord Kendrick again. Everything had been turned upside down today, and for some unfathomable reason, he was the only person who could soothe my worries.

I threw myself backward across the bed and stared up at my bedroom ceiling. Candles were lit, and shadows flickered across its surface. I considered ringing for the maid and going to bed early. Perhaps Aunt Augusta would speak to me again tomorrow.

But I couldn't make myself sit up. Instead, I continued to stare up at the ceiling and tried not to picture Auntie's expression. At times like this, her resemblance to my mother was quite inconvenient. I hated disappointing her, even though my current situation wasn't one of my making.

I rolled onto my side and tucked my legs onto the mattress. Logically, I knew that Auntie didn't blame me for what had happened. The debacle was all Henry's fault, after all. But Henry didn't seem to have a conscience, and he was probably out cavorting with Lord Penham. Heaven knows what type of trouble they were getting into. I just hoped that the next time he lost a gambling debt, he didn't see fit to scrawl my name on a piece of paper again.

A soft knock at the door startled me from my spiraling thoughts. I sat up on the edge of the bed to find Auntie opening the door.

She looked down at me. "We should talk about what happened."

I nodded and remained silent while she paced. Finally, after about a minute, she turned to me and took a deep breath. "We need a new plan."

I tilted my head and waited. She seemed to have already given this matter some thought and come to a decision. I needed to know what she was thinking before I could formulate my reply.

She settled next to me on the bed and turned to

look at me. With a soft smile, she tucked a strand of hair behind my ear. "You remind me so much of your mother."

I had to swallow back a sob. "I think the same thing every time I look at you. You and Mama are so similar. At times, I can almost pretend I haven't lost her."

Auntie shook her head. "She was much more carefree and adventurous than me."

That surprised me. "I never knew that."

Her smile held more than a hint of sadness. "It was always my biggest disappointment that I couldn't give my husband children. But between you and Henry, I always felt that at least our family line would continue. But now this whole mess with Lord Kendrick…" She shook her head. "We could leave London."

My heart began to race. This was exactly what I'd wanted a few short months ago. Unbelievably, Aunt Augusta was offering me the opportunity to go home and avoid the rest of the season.

"I know you didn't want to come to London and find a husband, but I thought I was doing the right thing by insisting." She clutched her hands in her lap and stared forward. "I shouldn't have forced you to come."

I covered her hands with mine and squeezed them. "You couldn't have known what Henry would do."

She shuddered and turned to look at me. "You truly don't want a husband?"

I shrugged. "Perhaps one day. I don't understand the hurry to wed before one is even twenty years of age."

She laughed. "This is such a mess. So be truthful, Caroline. Do you wish to return home?"

Part of me wanted to leap at her suggestion. I could return to my beloved Dorset. Last year had been so tranquil, going for long walks in the morning, practicing my mediocre skills at the pianoforte in the afternoon, reading, sewing little gifts for…

I frowned. I'd been sewing small blankets for the babies my acquaintances would one day have. I'd amassed quite a little collection of small gifts suitable to give a new mother. I'd left the monograms off, of course, telling myself I could add them once my friends started marrying and having babies.

But now, when I thought back to that drawer of blankets, a strange pang settled in my heart, and I came to an unexpected realization. I'd been sewing those blankets for my own future children. I just hadn't wanted to admit it.

"We could return next year," Auntie said, clutching my hands within both of hers. "Just say the word, and we'll return to Dorset. There will be speculation about our early departure, yes, but…" She sighed. "Nothing scandalous has happened so long as no one learns about that promissory note." She frowned. "Lord Kendrick won't say anything?"

I shook my head. "No, absolutely not. He just wants his winnings."

"So he won't reveal the truth. And you promised him that you'd pay what he's owed from your dowry."

I nodded. "It is sufficiently large that I will still have more than enough left over."

"Unless your brother decides to lose another gambling debt."

Now it was my turn to frown. "He can't give me away twice. Lord Kendrick has the prior claim, and I am not inclined to use the money my parents set aside for me to pay off all his gambling debts. Not when he has land and two estates."

Aunt Augusta smiled for the first time since entering the room. "Of course not. He's no longer a child and will need to learn to settle his own debts. *Especially* since he has so little concern for his sister's well-being."

I winced, but I couldn't deny the truth of her statement.

"So, tell me, Caroline. Are we leaving?"

I don't know why I didn't jump at the opportunity to say yes. No, that wasn't true. I knew exactly why. Lord Kendrick. I couldn't help thinking he'd be disappointed if I left London. Which was the height of foolishness. He wasn't interested in marrying me. For all I knew, he could be bedding another woman at that very moment.

I took a deep breath and met Auntie's gaze. "We are already here, and the season will be over soon enough. We might as well stay a little while longer."

Her entire face lit with joy, but her words held more than a hint of disbelief. "You want to stay."

I nodded. "Yes."

"Does your change of heart have anything to do with a certain Legendary Lord?"

I tried to ignore the heat creeping into my face. "Of course not. I'm surprised you think I'm that foolish."

She bumped her shoulder against mine. "You would hardly be the first woman to set her sights on an unattainable young man."

I turned to look at her, wondering what secrets

she hid. She'd shared so little about her personal life. "Lord Kendrick has no interest in marrying me."

A sly expression entered her eyes, and my heart began to beat faster because I knew exactly what she was going to say.

"Perhaps we can change his mind."

CHAPTER 23

CAROLINE

The next day, Lady Moreland called. We'd met earlier in the season, when she was still unmarried, but we hadn't formed a close friendship. The last I'd heard, she and her new husband had been away from town on their wedding trip.

Rumor had it that her father had arranged a match for her—followed closely by whispers that she had been ruined by Baron Moreland, one of the Legends. I'd been one of the few who hadn't believed those rumors. She'd always struck me as a dutiful young woman and not the type to engage in risky behavior.

But perhaps such things ran in the family. Her brother was also a Legend—the Marquess of Rexford. As I made my way to the drawing room to greet her, I couldn't help remembering the speculation that had taken place under this very roof when many of the eligible young women in town for the season had visited en masse. I was of the mind that her marriage to Baron Moreland came about because of his long acquaintance with her brother. They'd probably known each other for some time before deciding to marry.

She was standing by the drawing room's front windows, gazing out onto the street. When I entered the room, she turned to face me. Victoria Moreland was one year younger than me, but I'd always been struck by how composed and mature she seemed. Looking at her now, it was impossible to miss the happiness she exuded. Perhaps her marriage had been a love match after all.

Her dark hair was up in an elegant chignon, and her blue eyes almost gleamed with amusement. I couldn't understand why I'd been named the diamond this season when she'd also been newly out in society.

I dipped into a small curtsy. "It is a pleasant surprise to see you here. I've asked the staff to prepare refreshments."

She smiled warmly at me. "Lady Fredricks was gracious enough to invite me."

I wanted to groan. What exactly was Auntie planning?

I waited for her to take a seat on the settee before joining her. There was something in the way she was examining me that left me unsettled.

At a loss for what to say, I chose to be direct. "I'm surprised to see you here. I'd heard that you were on your wedding trip. My felicitations on your marriage, Lady Moreland."

She sighed, a blissful look coming over her face. "Yes, the trip was wonderful, but far too short."

I was surprised by the pang of envy I felt. What would it be like to be happily married? I couldn't fathom it. I certainly didn't have anyone who could put that dreamy look in my eyes. No one who actually wanted to marry me, that is. I *was* beginning to suspect that Kendrick would be capable of accomplishing that feat.

"Did Lord Moreland need to return to London on business?"

She shook her head, her smile holding a hint of

something I couldn't name. "Not exactly. We decided to return after my brother sent word about the situation in which you and Viscount Kendrick now find yourselves."

I winced. "I wasn't aware that information was widely known."

She put a hand on my arm. "Oh, no, not at all. The Legends are very strict about keeping their secrets. But…" She shrugged. "They are as close as family and are very loyal to each other. If one of them is in need of assistance, a call goes out to all of them."

Her words sent a thread of alarm through me. "I'm not a threat to Lord Kendrick."

She shook her head. "I might have chosen my words poorly. I meant that if anything of note happens to one, then word spreads among them. They take care of each other."

I couldn't help but wonder what that would be like since my own brother by blood was more concerned with taking care of himself. He'd had absolutely no qualms about handing me over to settle a gambling debt. That wasn't the behavior of someone who cared about his family.

"How much were you told?" I asked.

"I don't know any of the details. Just that your

brother gave you to Lord Kendrick after losing at cards." She leaned forward. "So, what does that mean?"

"Not what you're thinking."

She smiled. "What am I thinking?"

I laughed. If anyone could understand what it felt like to be mixed up with one of the Legends, it was this woman. And since I had no other allies aside from Kendrick, I decided to confide in her. Her brother was a Legend, and she'd married another one. Like my friend Diana, Victoria Moreland would know how to keep a confidence.

I explained everything to her. How Lord Penham had made it clear for the past year that he wanted to marry me and that I had no desire to marry him. How I'd managed to avoid coming out last year, but that Aunt Augusta had dragged me to London this spring. She already knew that had led to me being crowned the diamond of the season.

She shook her head. "You could have anyone. Before your brother's actions—" her face crinkled with disgust "—was there anyone else you wanted to marry?"

I sighed. "No, actually. I don't wish to marry at all."

Her eyes widened and her mouth dropped open. "No one?"

I shook my head.

"What about Lord Crandle or Lord Worth?"

I shrugged. "They're handsome enough."

"But…"

I shook my head. "Nothing. I feel nothing when I'm with them."

She looked away. "Perhaps that is a good thing."

I narrowed my eyes, trying to understand what she meant.

She must have seen my confusion, because she went on to ask, "What do you know about the marriage bed?"

Her question took me by surprise. "I know the barest details about what's involved. It sounds unpleasant."

Her smile was soft. "When you're with someone you care about, the opposite is true."

I couldn't help thinking about the way Kendrick had kissed me and how some instinct I hadn't known I possessed had come to life when his arms were around me. Beyond that kiss… I couldn't imagine it.

But since I was confiding in Victoria, perhaps I could ask for her advice. After all, I was sure that was why Auntie had invited her. "He hasn't admitted it, but Kendrick and I believe that my brother was hoping Kendrick would ruin me. And then Penham, with whom my brother is very close, would be able to swoop in and rescue me."

Her mouth tightened into a disapproving line. "What is it with men trying to force us into marriages we don't want?"

I nodded in agreement. "Lord Penham is so smug. It's insufferable." I tried to imagine having to endure the marriage bed with him, but my mind shied away from picturing that ordeal. I shuddered.

Victoria was watching me carefully now. "What exactly is happening between you and Lord Kendrick?"

"Nothing." I tried to keep my tone neutral, but the look on her face made it clear she didn't believe me.

"Nothing?"

"Nothing of note. We have formed an alliance of sorts."

That got her interest. She leaned a little closer. "Tell me about this alliance."

"Well, when I reach my age of majority, I will be able to take control of my dowry."

"Is that customary?"

I shrugged. "I don't know, but my parents set it up that way."

"Perhaps they didn't trust your brother."

"Aunt Augusta said the same thing. If they thought they couldn't trust him to take care of me, then they would have wanted to ensure I had a means of taking care of myself. But still, I'm sure they didn't think I would want that money for my independence instead of to secure a husband."

"No. They probably wanted to ensure that you made a good match. You are very beautiful, and I can certainly understand why you were named the diamond."

I forced back the urge to protest, since I knew very well what people saw when they looked at me. "I wish it had been someone else. In fact, I'm surprised it wasn't you."

She shook her head. "It matters not. We need to think about what we're going to do now."

"Lord Kendrick is going to keep other men away from me, and when I come into my inheritance, I shall pay off the debt my brother owes him."

She tilted her head. "How old are you now?"

I sighed. "It is still more than a year away, but I don't think he's in dire need of that money."

"Does your brother hope to have some of that money for himself?"

"I think so, but he has other assets. And he needs to learn to stop gambling away what he has."

She leaned a little closer. "So, your alliance with Viscount Kendrick—tell me, how do you feel about him?"

I could easily see him in my mind's eye. His dark brown hair framed a face that would have most women swooning, and his blue eyes always held a hint of amusement. He had an air about him that had one thinking he was on the verge of doing something outrageous that would have tongues wagging.

He could have any woman he wanted. What a pity he was determined to remain a bachelor. "He doesn't want to marry me."

She shook her head. "No, I don't believe he would. He had an encounter with his mistress earlier this year."

A pang of irrational jealousy went through me. "What type of encounter?"

"Do you read *The Mayfair Chronicle*?"

I shook my head. "No. Should I?"

"There is a column written by an anonymous

author who likes to speculate on the latest gossip surrounding the Legends."

"Well, that explains why everyone talks about them. They have to get their information from somewhere."

She nodded. "Kendrick's last mistress let it be known that he intended to marry her, and that story made it into the column."

My mouth dropped open, and a strange feeling in my stomach left me unsettled for a moment. "Was that true?"

Victoria shook her head. "No, but she was hoping to force his hand."

I couldn't help laughing at the woman's ridiculous attempt, and Victoria joined me.

"It was the height of foolishness," she said after a moment.

I sobered suddenly. "If she knew him at all, she wouldn't have bothered."

Victoria's expression turned sad. "I don't know him very well, but I imagine that experience was enough to sour him on the idea of marriage."

"Well, it's a good thing I'm not looking to marry." I forced myself not to look away.

"My husband wasn't looking to marry either."

I shook my head. I refused to allow myself to

consider what she seemed to be implying. To do otherwise would only lead to heartbreak.

Victoria's gaze was steady. "I believe we should get to know each other better. I'd like to keep an eye on this situation myself."

I could certainly understand why Moreland had fallen in love with this woman. I liked the idea of becoming friends, which meant I needed to be completely honest with her. "I believe that my aunt invited you here today hoping to entice you to promote a match between me and Viscount Kendrick."

She smiled softly at me. "I can't force him to do anything he doesn't want to do."

"I wouldn't want you to. And I have no illusions that he'll want to marry me."

She nodded firmly. "Whatever happens, it is always good to have additional allies. At the very least, I can help keep you safe from Lord Penham."

I smiled widely and rang the bell for tea. "I will never say no to another ally."

CHAPTER 24

KENDRICK

Satisfaction filled me as I entered Almack's. The emotion wasn't one I'd ever expected to feel, but tonight I wasn't alone. Heads turned when the seven of us—the six Legends and Victoria, Moreland's new bride—walked into the building as a group.

Rexford had carefully crafted the affectation several years ago to draw the maximum amount of attention whenever the Legends attended an event together. And it succeeded every time.

Conversation stopped, and every eye turned to

watch our progress. The scene would have been annoying if it wasn't so comical.

We made our way to the base of the stairs before turning to scan the people loitering in the area. When confronted with our perusal, they averted their eyes. I was aware of several matrons sneaking glances at Moreland's bride. They were clearly shocked that she'd been accepted into our fold. No doubt they'd assumed we'd only tolerate her and never expected us to include her in one of our rare joint appearances.

We turned and proceeded up the stairs.

The onlookers probably thought we'd made an exception for her because she was Rexford's sister. But the truth was that we all liked Victoria. She wasn't silly or vain and had blended seamlessly into the group, even if there were some things we could never discuss in her presence.

To be honest, I couldn't imagine the same welcome being given to the women the rest of us dallied with. But perhaps once we married as well… I forced my thoughts away from that line of thinking. The rest of us wouldn't be marrying for some time, so why was I thinking about future brides?

When we reached the next floor, we made our

way to the ballroom. As if my thought of future wives had summoned her, my gaze fell immediately on Caroline and her aunt when we entered the large room. The space was, of course, already packed with glittering guests, all dressed in their best finery.

Rexford greeted the patronesses and thanked them for the vouchers they'd supplied. Despite their advanced ages and stature in society, they turned into simpering women when subjected to his charm.

I took in the men hovering near Caroline, a smile curving my lips when I saw that her brother wasn't among them. When Rexford had secured the tickets and vouchers for tonight—after Fairfax had convinced him an appearance at Almack's would be amusing—he'd only obtained extras of each for Caroline and Lady Fredricks.

Caroline saw us right away, of course. A quiet arrival was impossible when we attracted so much attention.

Our eyes met across the room, and I inclined my head in greeting. Her smile widened before she turned to say something to her aunt.

Fairfax nudged me discreetly. "That's your cue."

I spared him a frown, annoyed that he was

enjoying this so much, before breaking off from the others. Moreland was already escorting his wife onto the dance floor, and I imagined the rest, aside from Rexford, would be escaping to the card room before long. They'd only come with me as a show of support. A reminder to everyone here tonight that our bond was unbreakable.

Rexford would probably be returning to King's soon. His appearance here served a second purpose—to help him uncover the identity of the anonymous author of the gossip column that reported on our exploits with alarming regularity.

One of the men standing near Caroline and Lady Fredricks moved to join them. No doubt his intention had been to ask Caroline for a dance. When one of the others caught his arm and inclined his head in my direction, the man wisely changed his mind and returned to his friends.

Apparently, Lady Fredricks was correct that my attention toward Caroline was hampering her ability to find a husband. I smiled in satisfaction at the knowledge. That meant our plan was working.

I joined them and addressed Lady Fredricks first, taking it as a good sign she wasn't ushering Caroline away as though I was a villain in a bad comedy. "I assume it is safe to approach."

She arched one brow. "You played your hand well, my lord."

I tilted my head. "In what way?"

"The vouchers for Almack's, of course."

"I'm surprised the two of you weren't invited by Lady Jersey herself."

I'd asked Mr. Clarence, who was club secretary at King's and Rexford's right-hand man, to look into the matter. Between him and Rexford, the pair had contacts everywhere. It had come as a shock to learn that Caroline had yet to be granted an invitation.

She shrugged. "I asked my nephew to look into the matter, but his attention has been elsewhere of late."

We both knew she was referring to his current campaign to gamble away his inheritance. I was surprised Lady Fredricks hadn't possessed enough influence herself, especially since Caroline was the diamond.

When I turned to Caroline, I couldn't keep my smile from widening. "I'm amazed you're not already dancing, Miss Edwards."

She sighed. "We've only just arrived, but I fear my card is almost full." Her voice lowered. "I did manage to save a dance for you. But given how those gentlemen are looking at me, I don't think I'll be standing here for much longer."

"Perhaps I should let it be known that I'm very unhappy with all the attention you're receiving."

"Don't you dare," Lady Fredricks said. "Not unless you intend to propose marriage yourself."

I noticed an air of calculation in her eyes, but I chose to ignore it. We'd already discussed this matter, after all.

Lady Fredricks looked past me. "Oh, look, there's Lady Henderson. I need to speak to her. I assume the two of you will be safe here until Caroline's next partner comes to collect her."

"Of course," I said.

We were in the middle of a crowded ballroom, after all. There wasn't true privacy to be had at Almack's, but there were several alcoves around the perimeter of the room that would permit us to escape unwanted stares. They wouldn't provide complete seclusion but would allow us to converse in private. And since we would still be visible to anyone walking by, our retreat wouldn't cause a scandal.

Lady Fredricks glanced at her niece, and something passed between them before she walked away.

I held out my arm to Caroline, who tucked her

hand into my elbow. We progressed around the outer perimeter of the room, looking for an unoccupied alcove. This early in the evening, it didn't take us long to find one, and the alcove was even partially obscured by a column.

Caroline sat on the bench and let out an annoyed sigh.

"My apologies," I said, taken aback by the sound. "If you wish to return—"

"Oh, no, not at all. Please sit."

I glanced at the space beside her. We wouldn't be touching, but we would be very close. "Are you certain?"

"If anyone wants to gossip about the fact you are sitting next to me in a public assembly room, where it is quite evident we are merely conversing, they are welcome to do so."

I nodded and sat next to her on the bench.

"What is the matter?" I had to admit I was concerned since it was obvious Caroline was unsettled.

She looked away, and I waited. Finally, she let out a breath and turned to face me again. "I think Auntie is under the impression that you'll change your mind and decide you want to court me."

I laughed, and she joined me.

"It is ridiculous."

I shrugged. "I can imagine why she'd think so. After all, I will need to marry one day."

She shook her head. "But not now." She looked away again. "It matters not because I won't be marrying either. Perhaps, several years from now, if we are both still unattached, we can have this conversation again."

I frowned, but not because her suggestion was unpleasant. No, I realized that I very much hated the idea of not seeing her for several years after this season. "What do you plan to do when you leave London?"

"I'll return home, of course, and I'll do what I can to avoid all the local suitors."

I was scowling now. "You have local suitors?"

She laughed. "Of course I do. They are every-where. I cannot avoid them, and they are most annoying."

I leaned closer. "Am I annoying?"

She met my gaze and shook her head. "You are the only gentleman who isn't."

The strains of a waltz began to play.

She sighed. "I believe I promised this dance to Lord Danbury. You were too late to save me from that ignominy."

I stood and held my hand out to her. "Allow me to come to your rescue, then."

She rose to her feet and glanced past me. Her voice was low when she said, "He's hovering right there."

I turned to face him. "My apologies, but I believe Miss Edwards forgot that I had already claimed this dance."

"I was so overcome by your request, my lord. I completely forgot to write down your name."

I turned back to her. "You can make it up to me now."

She dipped into a curtsy, a small, pleased smile on her lips as she took my hand. I swept her into my arms and waltzed with her to the center of the room.

She laughed. "That is twice now that you have stolen me from an unwanted dance partner. If only you were around all the time."

I didn't reply, but I found myself wishing for that as well. Moreland and Victoria were near, and I couldn't help but notice the way Victoria kept glancing over at us.

Caroline sighed. "My aunt has been playing matchmaker. She's already tried to elicit Lady Moreland's assistance."

I shook my head. "Well, Lady Fredricks needn't have bothered. I wouldn't be surprised to learn Victoria was already trying to play matchmaker for all of us." I nodded toward the other end of the room where Fairfax was dancing with a young woman. "He usually limits his dance partners to widows. Victoria must have introduced them, and I'm sure he felt obliged to ask her to dance."

Caroline giggled, and I smiled down at her, delighted by her amusement.

"You poor man," she said. "One woman admitted within the ranks of the Legends, and now you're not safe from anyone."

"Well, it's not as though we dislike the company of women. I would say the opposite is true."

She shook her head. "I'm sure it is."

CHAPTER 25

CAROLINE

It was nice to pretend. I'd never been one to fantasize about finding my prince charming or falling in love. I'd always hated the amount of attraction my appearance garnered when I was still barely out of the schoolroom.

I shouldn't have been surprised. My mother was beautiful, and she'd always seemed like a fairytale princess to me. Growing up, many had remarked on how much I resembled her. But when I turned fifteen, that attention became all-encompassing.

Older men who were happily married with daughters or granddaughters of their own were generally safe, for the most part. But the attention I attracted from young and middle-aged men was insufferable. Being named the diamond of the season had only intensified the attention.

But everything was different when I was with Kendrick.

I dropped into a curtsy when the waltz came to an end, enjoying the way he smiled down at me before bowing in a formal manner. One corner of his mouth tilted up, and I could tell he was amused by the performance. He was not a proper gentleman courting a young lady.

And I was not a foolish, naive young woman who thought he would be interested in marrying me. But for now, I would allow myself to enjoy the fantasy. I'd chastise myself about it later and give myself a stern talking to when I returned home. But while we were at Almack's, I could pretend he was courting me in earnest.

The rest of the evening wasn't nearly as enjoyable. Kendrick disappeared, and I assumed he had left. He'd already danced with me, so there was no reason for him to stay. I saw no gardens for us to disappear into. No secret rooms where we could breathe and laugh at all the antics of the young women and men who were here tonight. I'm not sure why he'd sent the vouchers and tickets for tonight's outing, but Auntie had been overjoyed to receive them, and the overture had gone a long way to thawing her suspicions about Kendrick's attention.

Several hours passed, and people were starting to leave for the night when I glimpsed Lord Penham. I turned away, smiling widely at the man who'd asked me for this last dance. At least my brother's friend hadn't arrived early enough to claim a dance with me.

I couldn't imagine why he was here now, since he wasn't the type to attend Almack's. Henry must have told him we'd be here. I'd known Penham's presence was a possibility but had assumed he wouldn't be granted entrance. I seemed to have underestimated his influence.

The dance was over far too quickly. In a simple quadrille, I did not have to engage in much small talk with my partner. But he was giving me that earnest look that told me he would be calling tomorrow.

I sighed and thanked him for the dance. He escorted me back to my aunt, and I stiffened when I saw that Penham was with her.

"Look who's here, Caroline," my aunt said.

"Lord Penham was hoping to have a dance with you."

My smile was insincere, and I couldn't help wishing that Kendrick was still here. "It is too bad the dancing is over."

As if I'd conjured him, Kendrick appeared at my side. "As promised, I brought you refreshments."

He handed me a cup of the weak tea Almack's was known for. He also had a cup for my aunt, who smiled warmly at him.

I watched her carefully when she turned to look at Lord Penham. She made a comment about the unseasonably warm weather that evening, attempting to engage him in conversation. But from the way Penham was looking at Kendrick, I could tell he was angry.

A shiver of foreboding slid down my spine. I didn't know why, but I had a horrible feeling something bad was going to happen.

"I am very tired, Auntie. I think it's time to go home." Smiling my thanks at Lord Kendrick, I drained the rest of the tea and handed the cup to a passing footman.

Kendrick moved between me and Lord Penham and held out his arm. Relieved, I tucked my hand into his elbow and leaned into him.

"Thank you, my lord." I lowered my voice so only he could hear. "I'd assumed you left hours ago."

He looked down at me. "I was passing the time in the card room, but it was always my intention to return. I wouldn't want you to think I'd abandoned you." He leaned a little bit closer. "Has Penham been bothering you?"

I shook my head and mouthed, "He only just arrived. I believe."

He nodded in satisfaction, and I realized he was serious about protecting me from the man's attention.

We made our way downstairs. Penham was escorting my aunt, and Kendrick and I followed a few steps behind them.

When we reached the main floor, Auntie asked a footman to call for our carriage. We made an awkward foursome standing there outside Almack's as we waited for the carriage to arrive. With each passing second, I could see Penham's temper growing.

I turned slightly and made sure my face was averted so that Penham wouldn't see me mouth the words to Kendrick. "Be careful. I think he's angry."

Kendrick nodded, but he didn't seem particularly concerned. Men were so frustrating. Although I didn't know why I was worried. What exactly was Penham going to do? They weren't going to brawl out in the street—not over me. Kendrick certainly wasn't emotionally invested enough for that. And he had arrived with his friends. If they were still here, Penham would be a fool to try anything.

Our carriage pulled up, and Kendrick helped me in before turning to help my aunt. He effectively blocked Penham from doing anything except standing ineffectually behind him.

"Thank you for tonight," my aunt said. "It was an unexpected surprise, and I do appreciate the effort you went to."

He smiled at her. "It was no effort at all. You need only ask if there is anything you need."

Auntie looked between him and me, an assessing gleam in her eye. She nodded her thanks, then Kendrick closed the door. She waited until the carriage pulled away before saying, "That young man is very fond—and protective—of you."

I wasn't sure what I felt at her words. Surprise? Pleasure? Shock? She didn't seem particularly upset about the revelation.

I shrugged. "We are friends. It stands to reason that he would be fond of me."

She smiled but said nothing more on the subject.

I resisted the urge to protest whatever it was she was thinking. The more I objected, the more she'd realize I liked Lord Kendrick more than I should. More than was wise, certainly.

CHAPTER 26

KENDRICK

The carriage drove away, and I turned to face Penham, who was still there. I'd hoped he would scurry off to whatever corner he'd come from, but I was not so fortunate. I stood my ground and waited for him to spout whatever nonsense was festering inside him.

The firm set of his jaw told me just how angry he was. *Good.* Men who were angry were careless. I'd promised Caroline that I would protect her from Penham above all others, and knowing what I did about him, I would see that promise through.

"You need to stop whatever it is you're doing with Miss Edwards."

I tilted my head. "You mean the woman your friend gave me?"

His jaw clenched, and in that moment, I became certain Caroline's brother had concocted this scheme with Penham.

"I've spoken to Weston, and we've come to an agreement. I am willing to pay you the money that was owed if you destroy the promissory note."

I took out my pocket watch and glanced at it, knowing the small delay was making him even angrier. I tucked it away again and faced him, a lazy drawl in my voice. "I've already been paid."

Penham's fists clenched at his sides, and I readied myself to ward off a blow. But what came instead took me by surprise. "The lot of you have always been insufferable. It's time someone taught you a lesson. You've left me no choice but to meet you at dawn."

Damn. This man was more foolhardy than I'd thought. He'd always managed to get himself into one scrape or another, but I'd never heard of him challenging anyone to a duel.

I smiled. "If you insist."

He nodded then turned to storm away. Fairfax

and Clifton melted out of the doorway to Almack's. From their expressions, I knew they'd overheard our exchange.

Fairfax whistled. "Are you going to kill him?"

Heaven knows I wanted to, but instead I forced myself to shrug. "That would be far more trouble than he is worth."

Clifton nodded. "So you'll wound him?"

"Of course."

"You could just accept the money," Fairfax said. "It's what you wanted that first night."

I shook my head. "I promised Caroline that I would keep her safe from Penham."

Clifton laughed. "So now you're her hero?"

Fairfax made a strangled sound of amusement.

"Hardly. But I do keep my word."

They both nodded. That was the one thing sacrosanct among us. It didn't matter whether we'd made a promise to each other or to a woman who was thrust into our midst. Once we gave someone our word, nothing would cause us to break it.

Fairfax nodded toward Clifton. "You'd better ask him to be your second. Much as I'd love to see Penham taken down, I don't think I have the gravitas required for such a role."

I nodded in agreement.

Fairfax liked to cultivate his air of being just a pretty face and a sly wit. We all knew there were depths beneath his surface, but for whatever reason, he liked to concentrate on the lighter side of things.

Clifton blew out his breath. "I suppose I need to track down Weston now since he'll be Penham's second."

"I'll make it up to you," I said.

"See that you do," Clifton said.

I nodded. It was what we did. Above all else, we were there for each other. No one kept score of who owed whom a favor because we didn't have to.

I turned and headed toward King's. Fairfax fell in step beside me. Almack's was only a short walk from Rexford's club, so I hadn't brought my carriage. We were just steps away from the club when Fairfax spoke again.

"Is she worth all this trouble?"

"Yes." My answer had been instant.

He nodded. "Well, I suppose there's going to be a duel tomorrow morning, then." He was clearly aiming for levity, but his slight frown reflected his concern.

I didn't know how good Penham was at pistols, but his skill didn't matter. I was better.

CHAPTER 27

CAROLINE

My pleasant dreams lasted through the night.

Then my maid woke me far too early the next morning. "A note has arrived for you, Miss Edwards. I didn't want to wake you, but I was assured you needed to read it as soon as possible."

Confused, I turned over to look at the clock on my bedside table. It was only five o'clock in the morning, and from her disheveled appearance, my maid had also been dragged out of bed.

I sat up and took the folded note from her with shaking hands. Everyone knew that bad news came in the middle of the night. But what confused me most was that the note hadn't been delivered to my aunt or to my brother. Remembering how I'd left Kendrick with an angry Penham last night, worry assaulted me.

My name was written in a flowery script, suggesting the note had been sent by a woman. The penmanship wasn't in Auntie's hand, however. I tore open the seal, took a deep breath, and unfolded the paper.

Caroline,

I thought you'd want to know that Lords Kendrick and Penham will be dueling this morning at 6 a.m. I don't know if it can be stopped, but I've asked my carriage driver to wait after delivering this note. He will take you where you need to go.

Victoria Moreland

I stared at the note for several seconds, my sluggish brain trying to make sense of the words. Surely this couldn't be true. Kendrick wasn't foolish enough to issue such a challenge. He had other ways of gaining the upper hand with Penham.

I closed my eyes as the truth hit me. This was exactly the kind of thing Penham would do. And that meant my brother would also be there to act as his second. Why were the two of them insisting on making this situation even worse? They were the ones who'd set this whole ordeal into motion, and now Penham was calling out Lord Kendrick, who'd also been an unwitting pawn in their scheme.

Anger, swift and hot, rose within me, and I turned to my maid. "I need to leave at once. The most practical clothes for such an early hour."

She nodded. "I will accompany you."

"Thank you, Milly." I scrambled from the bed and turned to face her. "Is my brother here?"

She shook her head. "He didn't come home last night. Should I inform Lady Fredricks about what is happening?"

I shook my head. "My aunt does not need to know about this. It will only worry her. And I'm sure Henry will already be waiting."

She nodded, no doubt relieved to learn that I'd be meeting my brother. She didn't need to know that Henry wouldn't be expecting to see me this morning. In fact, I could guarantee he'd be very annoyed when I showed up.

I dressed quickly, and the two of us made our way downstairs, taking care to move quietly so we wouldn't wake Auntie. I told the lone footman waiting in the hallway that I was going to meet my brother. It wasn't strictly a lie since Henry would be there.

"I'll have the carriage readied," he said.

"There's no need." I opened the front door and looked into the street. "Ah yes, the carriage waited. It will take me to my brother."

I gave him a smile that I hoped would reassure him that there was nothing to worry about, then Milly and I left the house. The driver jumped down to help us into the carriage, then we were on our way.

"It's a duel, isn't it?" Milly asked.

I hesitated, but then I nodded. When we reached our destination, she would see for herself what was happening.

"Is it wise for you to be there?"

"I don't know," I said with a sigh. "But they're dueling because of me. If there is even a chance that I can stop it, I need to try."

Milly didn't seem mollified, but she didn't protest again.

With every minute that passed, my anger at Henry and Penham turned into something else. Bone-deep fear. What if they hurt Kendrick? I didn't really know anything about duels, just that they rarely happened nowadays. But I did know that even a minor wound could fester and become infected.

I closed my eyes and sent up a prayer to whatever angels liked to watch over the foolhardy men in our lives. I didn't want Lord Penham to be hurt, of course, but if only one of them could come out of this safely, I would choose Kendrick.

My prayers were a mantra in my head. *Please don't get hurt, Kendrick. And don't die.*

I couldn't conceive of a world where the charming, attractive, smart, and utterly enticing man who'd danced with me last night and who'd saved me on more than one occasion could be mortally injured.

When the carriage drew to a halt, I flung open the door and jumped down. "What direction?" I shouted up at the driver..

"The field over there. Please be careful."

I nodded, lifted my skirts, and raced in the direction he'd indicated.

I stopped when I saw them, my heart sinking when I realized I was too late. They were already facing away from one another and pacing away. I was frozen in place, my heart in my throat. I wanted to rush into the clearing, but what if my outburst distracted Kendrick? I wouldn't be able to live with myself if I was responsible for causing him harm. He was already in enough danger because of me.

I didn't want to see the scene play out, but I was powerless to look away. My brother stood off to one side, the Earl of Clifton at his side. The seconds. The rest of the Legends were standing on the other side of the field, watching the event unfold.

My gaze moved to Henry, who was counting their paces. When he reached ten, I stiffened. They were still too close. Penham wouldn't miss.

He continued counting until fifteen. Then, in a blur of movement, Kendrick and Pelham pivoted, took aim, and fired.

The shock of the pistols firing had me moving. Without waiting to see whether he'd been hurt, I lifted my skirts again and raced to Kendrick's side.

CHAPTER 28

KENDRICK

We stood like that for what seemed an eternity. Then Penham looked down at his right shoulder, where blood was seeping through the layers of his clothing. His eyes lifted to meet mine before swiveling to the left.

I followed his gaze to see someone racing across the field.

Caroline.

My stomach clenched as I waited to see whether she'd go to him. Women were such delicate crea-tures, after all. And I might have played right into

Penham's hands, allowing him to appear the wounded hero. Caroline came to a halt midway between Penham and me. Her jaw was tight, her breath coming in pants. She turned and walked toward me.

She stopped when she reached my side. "Are we done here?"

I nodded.

"Caroline—" Penham called out to her.

She whipped around and glared at him. "Enough of this nonsense. I don't know what you and my brother thought was going to happen here, but I am not impressed by your theatrics." She turned to me again, and I didn't miss the way her eyes swept up and down my body. She let out a relieved sigh when she saw I was uninjured. "I would appreciate it if you could escort me back to my carriage."

Silently, I offered her my arm. For a moment, I thought she was going to refuse it, but she finally relented and placed her hand in the crook of my elbow. I nodded to my friends, who were watching the scene unfold from the side, and led her to where my carriage was waiting. We'd already reached it when she realized the direction we'd been headed.

She was definitely more upset than she was willing to let on.

"This isn't my carriage."

"No, but I can see you're distraught. Please allow me to escort you home."

Her eyes searched mine. "I came in Lord Moreland's carriage… And my maid is waiting for me."

"Moreland is here. He'll take care of it."

She hesitated, unsure. Finally, she nodded and allowed me to help her into the carriage. I instructed my driver to take us to Caroline's home first, then I joined her, settling onto the bench opposite her.

Heavy silence blanketed the air, and I watched as Caroline stared down at her clenched hands. When she'd said nothing for a full minute, I could no longer take the quiet.

"I'm sorry you had to witness that."

When she looked up, I saw her lower lip tremble. I wanted to curse but somehow stopped myself. "Penham will be fine. It was only a shoulder wound."

She reached across the carriage and hit my arm. "You could have been hurt. What were you thinking?"

Her statement took me aback. "I was thinking that I'm not the type of man to run away from a challenge." I rose and moved to sit next to her.

She glared at me. "Penham is a fool. I wouldn't have cared if you refused his challenge."

"But I care. I can't have people thinking me a coward."

She hit my arm again. "Heaven forbid people think you a coward. If you had died out there, they would have said you'd gone foolishly to your grave, but at least you acted bravely."

I examined her face, taking note of the taut line of her jaw, the way she pressed her lips together, and something shifted in my chest.

"Caroline," I asked slowly, "were you worried about me?"

She huffed out a breath. "Of course I was worried about you."

"But you weren't worried about Penham or your brother, who acted as his second?"

"My brother was in no danger. And if he'd been hurt, it would have served him right."

I frowned. "What if he'd taken Penham's place against me? Penham wanted me to destroy the promissory note. An argument could be made that your brother also had a right to engage in the duel."

She snorted. "Henry isn't that brave, or that foolish. Penham, on the other hand, is." She shook her head. "And you…"

"What about me?"

She let out a breath. "I knew you wouldn't kill him or hurt him terribly. Although, you should have aimed for his leg. That would have kept him home for the rest of the season. As it is, he'll don a sling and wear that injury as a badge of honor. I can just imagine how he'll spin a tail about how he was hurt by a blackguard while trying to defend a woman's honor."

I stared at her, stunned. How was it possible that this woman cared more about me being injured than her own brother?

"You couldn't have known I wouldn't kill him."

She actually smiled. "You're a smart man, Kendrick. You know dueling is illegal, and you wouldn't draw that type of attention to yourself or your friends. It is one thing for people to turn a blind eye when someone receives a superficial wound, but it is quite another when someone is killed."

I shook my head. "How are you so clever when…"

She snorted. "When my brother is a lackwit?"

She laughed louder. "Apparently, I received all the intelligence in this family."

"And all the beauty," I said.

Her eyes met mine and held. In the short time I'd known Caroline, I'd watched her deflect comments about her beauty and change the subject. But she was so much more than what fools like Penham and the others saw when they looked at her. She was a woman any man would be honored to call his wife, and not just because she'd look pretty on his arm. If they looked deeper, they'd see how special she was. The thought terrified me.

She searched my features. "What are you thinking? You have a very strange expression." She licked her lips, and I wanted to groan. "Have you decided that I'm not worth all this trouble? Heaven knows I wouldn't blame you."

She looked away and leaned back against the seat cushion, crossing her arms over her chest.

The backs of my hands brushed against her breasts as I reached for her hands. She sucked in a shocked breath, her gaze flying to mine, but didn't protest when I captured her hands and held them between us.

"I'm thinking that, while your brother is a fool, he might have done me the biggest favor any man could do for another when he wrote your name on that note."

Her mouth dropped open and I waited to see what she would say. The air in the carriage seemed to thicken around us as we continued our slow progress through the streets.

Finally, she shook her head. "I don't understand what's happening here."

"The truth, my dear, is that it would have been a shame if we'd never met."

She licked her lips again, and I wanted nothing more than to draw her into my arms. But I wouldn't take advantage of her when she was still distraught. "I'm going to take you home now, Caroline. But you should know that I've decided we should get to know each other better."

She shook her head again. "You're not looking for a wife, and I'm not looking for a husband."

I dropped a kiss onto the center of one palm, enjoying the way she shivered. "But that doesn't mean we can't spend time together." My eyes were steady on hers. "I know you find me attractive. I also know that you want me to kiss you right now."

Her eyes fell to my mouth, and it took everything in me not to do just that. If she were any other woman, I would already be kissing her, but I wanted Caroline to come to me with full understanding of what I was proposing. I wouldn't force her, but I wanted her completely, and she needed to know that it was her choice. I didn't want her to have any regrets.

The carriage slowed, and I glanced out the window. "We're almost at your house."

She shook her head, and I felt the disappointment keenly. "No?"

She shook her head again. "No, I think I want to go to *your* home."

My blood turned thick in my veins. I should refuse. "Perhaps you need to think about this."

She leaned forward. Her mouth was only inches from mine. "I've thought about nothing else, and today showed me one thing. If something had happened to you on that field, if Penham had managed to hurt you or…" She shook her head as if unable to complete that thought. "If anything had happened, my one regret would have been not knowing what it was like to be with you."

She didn't need to say anything more. I was a weak man, after all.

I tapped on the roof of the carriage and leaned forward to open the small window that allowed me to speak directly to the driver. "There's been a change of plans. Take me home."

The carriage sped up then, and I turned to Caroline. "If you change your mind…"

She smiled, and the look in her eyes hit me square in the middle of my chest. "I'm not going to change my mind."

CHAPTER 29

CAROLINE

I hadn't lied when I told Kendrick I wanted to be with him, but that didn't mean I wasn't nervous. Was I really going to return with him to his house and allow him to make love to me? Because there could be no other reason he'd take me home with him.

The drive wasn't long, and I was surprised to find he had a townhouse in Mayfair. I realized I didn't know much about Kendrick, but surely he was financially sound if he possessed a home in the most fashionable district of London.

Kendrick held one of my hands, and he kept glancing at me throughout the drive. I knew he was checking to see whether I'd changed my mind. But when the carriage turned onto the street leading to the mews behind the houses, my nerves vanished.

I wanted to do this. No, I needed to do this. Kendrick was the only man I'd ever felt any romantic interest in. I wasn't foolish enough to think he'd want anything more than a brief liaison with me, but I did want to experience what it would be like to be with someone who made my heart beat faster.

He'd shown me time and time again that I could trust him. The Legends were notorious for their love affairs, but I'd never heard anyone say they didn't treat women well. Even now, I knew that if I changed my mind, he'd order the carriage to take me home. He was a rake, yes, but for now, he was *my* rake.

The carriage slowed to a halt, and silence stretched between us before Kendrick spoke. "Last chance to change your mind, Caroline."

I licked my lips and shivered when I saw the way his eyes narrowed in on the movement. "I haven't changed my mind."

He didn't bother to wait for a footman. I

watched him jump down from the carriage, fold down the stairs, and hold out his hand. There would be no turning back, but I smiled and placed my hand in his. Excitement coursed through me when his fingers tightened around mine. I was surprised by how much I wanted this.

Kendrick helped me climb down from the carriage and led me through a side door into his townhouse without another word.

When we reached the main hallway, his butler came into view. I noticed the way the man's eyes widened briefly when he saw me, before he composed his expression.

"All is well, I assume?" Kendrick asked.

The butler nodded. "Nothing to report, my lord."

"Very well. Please see to it that we're not disturbed."

The butler inclined his head. "Yes, my lord."

My hand was still in Kendrick's as he led me up the stairs. Nerves assailed me again when an uncomfortable thought occurred to me. Kendrick was very experienced, and I wasn't. For the first time, I wondered if my inexperience would disappoint him.

"I suppose you do this often?"

He turned to look at me but didn't volunteer any information.

"Bring women back to your house, that is."

We turned down a short hallway, and he stopped before a bedroom door. He stared down at me. "You are the first."

I couldn't hold back an indelicate snort of disbelief. "I doubt that very much."

One corner of his mouth quirked. "You are the first woman I've brought home with me. Normally, I do this elsewhere."

That would explain why the butler's eyes had widened at the sight of me. If not for that, I wasn't sure I'd believe Kendrick. But I saw no reason for him to lie about this. It wasn't as though he was trying to convince me he was a chaste man.

"I'm not going to marry you."

I laughed. "I don't want you to."

His smile widened, and he opened the door to his bedchamber.

Having a brother, it wasn't the first time I'd been inside a gentleman's private rooms. I'm not sure what I expected to find when I crossed the threshold. An enormous bed, perhaps. Paintings of naked women.

I stood still, my gaze sweeping across the room.

An ordinary bed, not too dissimilar from the large bed in which my brother preferred to sleep. Dark wood furniture. Curtains and bedlinens that were dark-blue in color.

"It's so ordinary."

Kendrick laughed. "I don't think I want to ask what you were expecting."

My cheeks heated, embarrassment taking hold.

Before I could apologize for my unintended slight, he turned me to face him. His head lowered. "I'll have to make up for my *ordinary* furnishings."

Then he kissed me, and my thoughts scattered. The only thing that mattered was this man and the way his mouth felt against mine. He wrapped his arms around my waist and brought me fully against him, and my last remaining fears disappeared.

I circled my arms around his neck in an attempt to bring myself even closer. His tongue darted into my mouth when I opened for him, and the world beyond these walls receded. This was what it must feel like to be inebriated.

His scent filled my nostrils, and I wanted more. I was completely certain I'd made the right choice. A small part of my logical brain told me that after today I would never be the same, but I ignored that voice.

Kendrick was showing me that I wasn't completely unaffected by the male sex as I'd feared. Unfortunately, he would never offer me an honorable marriage. So I would content myself with being dishonorable with him.

I wasn't sure how long we continued wrapped up in each other's arms, our kisses becoming long and languorous. But when he pulled back and stared down at me, both of us were breathing heavily.

"Please tell me you know what's going to happen." There was a small line between his brows, and I resisted the urge to reach up and smooth away his worry.

I couldn't pretend to be like the other women he'd bedded, but I didn't want him to doubt that I was ready to be with him.

I nodded. "At the start of the season, I thought it prudent to ask someone to explain the details."

His brows rose at that. "Tell me you didn't speak to your aunt about this."

I smiled. "Heavens no. I asked some of the maids."

He was grinning now. "What was their reaction to your question?"

I couldn't help but laugh. "My lady's maid

refused to answer, and I had to beg her not to speak about my curiosity to my family. But then I began watching the way the maids behaved around the footmen. There were two who I could tell were quite happy with the attention some of the footmen gave them."

His eyes crinkled at the corners. "So you asked them?"

I nodded. "If I was going to be forced onto the marriage mart, I wanted to know what lay ahead."

He cupped my face then, his thumb caressing my bottom lip then moving along my cheek. He slid a hand behind my head, his fingers threading through my hair. "So you're aware of what I want from you?"

I brought my hands to his shoulders and dragged them down his arms to cup his elbows. "Yes."

He must have noticed the slight hesitation in my voice, because he frowned. "You've changed your mind?"

I felt his muscles tense, and I knew he was about to pull away.

I tightened my grip on his arms. "No. But I need you to tell me what you want me to do."

His brow smoothed. "You've never struck me as

the type of woman who likes being told what to do."

A shiver went through me at the way he seemed to delight in my words. "Normally, I'm not. But with you…" I licked my lips, and his eyes darted to my mouth. "With you and in this matter, I think I would like it."

His eyes roamed my face, then he nodded. This time, when he stepped back, I let him go.

"I would like you to disrobe for me."

My mind blanked at his words. I couldn't. Surely, such an act was indecent. But then I realized who I was with. Almost before realizing, I was reaching up to undo the top buttons at the back of my gown.

I couldn't undo all of them on my own. When I reached the point between my shoulder blades, I turned around and looked at him over my shoulder. "Much as I would love to do just that, there is a reason women have ladies' maids."

I didn't have to ask twice. He moved into place, and his fingers made quick work of the rest of the buttons. Then he unlaced my corset.

His movements were quick and efficient. I tried not to think about all the times he'd done this with other women. All that mattered was that he was with me now.

I turned around and shifted the fabric of my dress from my shoulders. It puddled on the floor around me. His eyes were dark as I also removed my corset and dropped it on the floor.

CHAPTER 30

KENDRICK

$\mathcal{I}$'d been in the presence of many beautiful women, but something about Caroline set her apart. As I watched her cast aside her corset and stand before me in her chemise like an angel just before her fall, I was struck with the sensation that I was on the precipice of something important. Something I'd never experienced before with a woman.

She trusted me.

Despite the fact that I'd made her no promises, that she was not the type of woman who engaged in casual dalliances, she'd chosen to give herself to me.

She was willing to risk everything to be with me today.

An uncomfortable emotion was trying to work its way into my consciousness, but I refused to allow it to surface. Nothing mattered except this moment with this incredible woman.

When she reached for the ribbon at the top of her chemise, just above her breasts, her fingers trembled. The hint of her nervousness made me feel unworthy of her trust. Her willingness to do what I'd asked of her was enough. I didn't need her to act the part of a more experienced woman.

"Stop."

She froze, and her eyes lifted to meet mine. "Am I doing something wrong?"

I closed the distance between us and covered her hands with mine. "You're perfect."

Truer words had never been spoken.

She leaned into me, and I couldn't resist kissing her again. Normally, I wasn't sentimental, but I wanted to show her as much pleasure as I knew she'd bring me. For some unknowable reason, this woman had me thinking about what I could do for *her*. It was a novel feeling and one I'd never experienced before.

I swept a hand under her knees and lifted her into my arms.

She wrapped her arms around my neck and pulled back to smile at me. "I must admit that I never expected you to actually sweep me off my feet."

I couldn't help laughing. "To be honest, you bring out something in me I didn't realize I possessed."

She bit her lip as she examined me. "Kendrick—"

I kissed her delectable mouth to stop the question I knew she wanted to ask. *What is happening here?* I didn't want to think about it, and I certainly didn't want her to speak of it aloud, because my answer would only disappoint her. And that was the last thing I wanted to do.

I carried her to the bed and laid her carefully on its surface. When I stepped back to look down at her, I couldn't help thinking she looked perfect reclining on my bed. I vowed then that I would bring no other woman here. Only Caroline.

I straightened and shrugged out of my tailcoat.

She shifted onto her elbows, her eyes moving up and down my body as I unbuttoned my waistcoat. It wasn't lust that I saw in her eyes, but wonder. She was as surprised by her reaction to me as I was shocked by my response to her.

I dropped my coat and waistcoat to the floor. My valet would chastise me for my carelessness later, but I couldn't fight my sense of urgency.

I tugged my shirt over my head, dropping it on top of the pile of clothing. Caroline's tongue darted out to lick her lips as she stared at me. We stayed like that for some time, her eyes taking in my shirtless form, my own gaze moving over her body. I could see the dark tips of her breasts plainly through her thin chemise, as well as the shadowed space between her thighs.

I don't think Caroline realized I could see so much through the thin white fabric, but I knew that it would be too much to ask her to lie naked for my perusal. That would come in time.

I hardened thinking about all the things I wanted to show her, to do with her and for her.

"Kendrick." Her voice was low and husky.

"I know, darling." I lay next to her, and she rolled into me. "Are you scared?"

She shook her head. "I should be, but no."

I waited for her to touch me first, delighting in the way her slim fingers moved over my arms and chest. When her hands strayed down to my abdomen, I couldn't hold back a soft grunt as I thought about how good it would feel to have her hands on my cock.

I rolled on top of her and kissed her, then I started moving down her body. Before long, I drew her chemise up her thighs, then she shifted her hips so I could remove it completely. Finally, my mouth was on her breasts.

She held me there, her fingers curling into the hair at the nape of my neck while she made soft, husky sounds that inflamed me further.

I moved down her body and made space for myself between her legs. I'd never done this for another woman, but Caroline was special. And I couldn't hold back the selfish desire to ensure she remembered me when we parted.

She hesitated before relaxing fully, a small crease forming between her eyebrows. "I wasn't told to expect this." Then she exhaled, her breath a soft hiss as I tasted her. "I don't know what you're doing, but please don't stop."

I chuckled against her then redoubled my efforts, enjoying the taste of her on my tongue. She began undulating her hips, which told me she was enjoying this as much as I was. I slid a finger inside her, groaning at how small she was, and concentrated on suckling at the small bundle of nerves at the top of her opening.

I was impatient now, eager to be inside her. But I wouldn't take her until she'd found her release. When I slid a second finger into her, relishing the tightness and anticipating how amazing she would feel when I finally slid into her, she made a soft cry of surprise, and her whole body shook. I kept my mouth on her until the last shudder raked through her body.

I dropped soft kisses on her inner thighs before moving over her again. Her pupils were blown wide, the blue almost completely gone now.

"I never imagined such a thing was possible."

I nuzzled her ear, delighting in the shiver that ran through her body, before licking her neck. I inhaled deeply, enjoying her scent and hoping it would permeate my sheets. "I want to do so much to you."

Her hands were on my waist, then she was reaching to undo the fall of my trousers.

I lifted my head to stare down at her. "You don't have to."

Her smile widened. "I want to do this."

I nodded, and she continued unbuttoning my

trousers. Then she reached inside and encircled my cock with her hand. I groaned as she explored me.

"I was told that men get hard," she said, "but I didn't expect you to also feel so soft."

"You're killing me, darling."

"I hope you mean that in a good way."

I watched her, my heart unexpectedly full. "I mean that in only the best way." I kissed her again, but I soon needed to place a hand on her wrist so she would stop. "If you keep doing that, we won't get to the best part."

She licked her lips. "We wouldn't want that."

"No," I agreed.

I was still wearing my trousers, but I couldn't wait any longer. I took myself fully out and placed the head of my cock at the entrance of her wet heat. I forced myself to wait a moment, allowing her to get used to the idea that I would soon be inside her.

"That feels so good," she said, her voice soft. "I wasn't sure it would."

"It's going to hurt when I get inside you."

She nodded. "I know."

I pushed into her with one quick thrust then held myself still when her breath caught. I kept my eyes on her face, and I hated the pain I could see reflected in the way she clenched her jaw.

I resisted the fleeting urge to apologize, since I wasn't sorry. She felt incredible. Doing this with Caroline… I didn't know why, but I'd never enjoyed a woman half as much.

A small vee formed between her brows. "Why are you waiting?"

I huffed out a small laugh. "I'm not a monster. I'm waiting for you to become more comfortable."

She shifted her hips, causing me to let out a surprised grunt. I moved slowly then, out and then in, and she made a soft sound that had me wanting to continue. But first, I had to ask, "Does it still hurt?"

Her hands were gripping my shoulders, but she lifted one to cup my cheek. "No, Kendrick. I think I'd very much like for you to continue."

She didn't need to ask twice. Holding back proved almost impossible, but it was important to me that she enjoy this. So I reached down to stroke her where our bodies were joined.

Her breath hitched, and she started to move. I allowed her to set the pace. When she tightened unexpectedly and reached her second peak, I was no longer myself. I pushed into her again and again until I reached my own release. I pulled out, but not as quickly as I should have. I was calling myself all sorts of names, but the look of wonder on Caroline's face made me pause.

"I think," she said, "I can understand why women are lining up to be your mistress."

I dropped next to her with a surprised laugh and pulled her into my arms. "You are not going to be my mistress, Caroline."

She let out a soft sigh, "I know. But it would have been nice."

CHAPTER 31

CAROLINE

"Caroline."

I snuggled deeper into Kendrick's side, enjoying his warmth and the way his arms tightened around me. This was the most pleasant dream I'd ever had.

"Darling," he murmured against my ear. His breath caused goose flesh to travel down my spine.

Blinking against the light, I opened my eyes and looked at him. His deep-blue eyes were fixed on me, a hint of amusement tilting one corner of his mouth.

"I love your eyes," I said, my voice rough from sleep.

He cupped my cheek and continued to stare at me. When his eyes flicked to my lips, I smiled. Yes, this was certainly the best dream I'd ever had.

"Much as I would love you to remain in my bed, we need to think about how you'll be going home."

I frowned, confused by his words. Why would Dream Kendrick be concerned about me going home? As clarity came to me, I turned away from him.

At some point, he must have gotten up to get a blanket because we were now underneath a coverlet, and we'd made love on top of his bed. My gaze flew to the window. Daylight still streamed in from outside, thank goodness, but I didn't know what direction his bedroom faced, so I had no idea what time it was. I sat up, clutching the blanket to my chest. "I must have fallen asleep."

"We both fell asleep."

He sat next to me, but I couldn't face him. What must he think of me? I was fairly certain Kendrick wasn't used to women making themselves quite so comfortable. No doubt a more sophisticated woman would have dressed immediately after making love and departed.

Embarrassment flooded through me as I worried about what he was thinking. Here I was, telling him I wasn't looking for a husband, then I fell asleep in his arms. Such behavior didn't befit someone only engaging in a casual liaison.

I met his indulgent gaze. "My apologies. I'll get dressed right away and leave."

I started to turn away, trying to work out whether I should wrap the blanket around myself as I gathered up my clothes. I spied what must have been his dressing room to the left, where I could duck in to change.

Before I could stand, Kendrick stopped me with a hand on my upper arm. "Caroline, what are you thinking right now?"

I closed my eyes, mortification sweeping through me. "You are correct. How long have we been here? If Henry returns home and I'm still missing, Aunt Augusta will worry."

I expected him to release me. Instead, he tugged on my arm, and I fell back onto the bed.

He leaned over me, his forehead creased with concern. "Please don't lie to me."

I stared up at him, and somehow, I knew what

he was thinking. I'd never felt the need to hide the truth from him before, and he was disappointed I was doing so now.

I sighed. "If you must know, I'm mortified and trying to hold onto my dignity."

He frowned. "Do you regret what happened?"

I closed my eyes, unable to look at him. "No, not at all. I just feel so very gauche right now. I know that a more worldly woman wouldn't have fallen asleep. She would have thanked you very prettily for a nice tumble and gone on her way."

His thumb traced my cheek then my lower lip. "Look at me, Caroline."

I swallowed and opened my eyes.

He was watching me carefully. "You're not just any woman. And if it's gauche to fall asleep, then I'm guilty of that sin as well."

Relief flooded through me that he wasn't angry or disappointed. "What time is it?"

"It is not yet noon. You've only been here a short while. But you are correct, you do need to get dressed. Unless you've changed your mind again and do want me to ruin your reputation."

I rose to sit, continuing to clutch the blanket to my chest. "I doubt it would dissuade Penham. But maybe the nonsense that took place today will change his mind."

He smiled, but there was a hint of darkness in his eyes. "Penham can't have you."

I might have imagined it, but I thought I detected a note of possessiveness in his tone. I liked the idea that he didn't want to see me with someone else. It was enough for now. I could pretend.

"I should get dressed. But I might need some help."

His grin widened. "By all means."

He sprang from the bed. He was still shirtless, but he wore his trousers. He must have buttoned them when he went to get the blanket. *Probably for the best.* I winced at the slight ache between my legs. I didn't think I'd be able to make love again so soon, much as I might want to.

He moved around the room, picking up my scattered items of clothing and laying them on the bed. I reached for my chemise and, after a deep breath for courage, dropped the blanket. Then I tugged the chemise over my head.

My back was turned to him, but I could almost feel the weight of his gaze on my body. Happiness filled me at the knowledge that he enjoyed looking at me. I turned around to face him. My gaze swept over him, trying to memorize every detail. I might never see him this way again.

He let out a frustrated breath. "Much as I'd love to keep you here all day, we need to get you home."

I nodded and faced away from him again while he laced me into my corset. Then I stepped into my dress, and he helped me with the buttons.

I looked around his room and frowned. "Do you not have a mirror? I need to fix my hair."

He disappeared into the changing room and returned with a small handheld mirror. He held it up for me as I did what I could to repair the mess we had made of my hairstyle. Finally, when I was presentable again, he set down the mirror, and I watched him dress.

He disappeared into the dressing room again and emerged with a freshly starched cravat. I watched him tie the complicated knots as though he'd trained as a valet himself. My brother had never managed that particular task.

When he was finished, we stood there, staring at one another.

"I—"

"You—"

We'd both spoken at the same time. He inclined his head and allowed me to go first.

"I need to find some way to sneak back into my house."

He tilted his head and examined me. "How did you know about the duel? Surely your brother didn't tell you."

"Moreland told his wife, and Victoria sent me a note. She guessed—correctly, I might add—that I would want to see if I could stop it."

He shook his head. "Of course he did."

"He was being a good friend to you."

"Oh, I know. But it's still strange that he has a wife now with whom he is clearly besotted."

I smiled. "They do make a lovely couple. Everyone was shocked when they learned about the wedding."

"Yes," Kendrick said. "It was a whirlwind affair, but it worked out well in the end." He seemed to consider the matter. "Since Moreland saw fit to interject himself and his wife into the duel, I don't think they'd mind if we paid them a visit now. Victoria can take you home in their carriage. And you wouldn't be lying if you told your aunt you were with her."

I nodded. "Thank you for being so kind and generous."

His eyes were fixed on my face. "I was surprised

that you were so worried about me. I don't think I know of another woman who would have cared if I'd been hurt."

I wanted to say so much, but I couldn't. Instead, I settled for a version of the truth. "We're friends, are we not? And friends worry about one another."

His smile was soft. "Yes, Caroline, I do believe we are friends. Now, let's get you home."

CHAPTER 32

CAROLINE

onvincing Auntie to stay home that
evening was surprisingly easy. I told her I
had a headache, and while I don't think she
believed me, she'd heard about my early outing—
that I'd gone to see Henry, who'd been out all night.
Her relief had been evident when I'd finally
returned home in the Morelands's carriage.

Thankfully, Baron Moreland had already
returned the carriage, saving us from having to
concoct another excuse. He wasn't home when
Kendrick dropped me off, which had been a relief. I

wasn't sure I could have faced him after leaving the dueling field with Kendrick.

Victoria had waited until Kendrick left before prying from me all the details about what had happened. I'd been reluctant at first, so she'd shared about her courtship with Moreland, that he'd been asked to act as her protector. The details were shocking, but the knowledge that she knew what it was like to care for a man yet have no expectation of marriage made me comfortable sharing what had happened with Kendrick.

"He won't marry you," she said when I reached the end of my story.

I sighed and looked away. "I know, but I wasn't looking for a husband, and he's already given me so much more than I ever expected I could have with a man. It will have to be enough."

Victoria had hugged me then sent me off in the carriage. Auntie had also hugged me when I'd arrived home.

After she'd ensured I was safe, she asked about Henry. "Please tell me that your brother is well. I've been so concerned about the two of you."

I nodded. "He was out all night with Lord Penham." That much, at least, was true. "I think they decided to return to Penham's townhouse."

Auntie frowned. "Where did you meet them?" She must have sensed my reluctance to reply, because she sighed and shook her head. "Never mind. It is enough that the two of you are safe."

She left me to my own devices after that, so I had the rest of the day to daydream about what had happened between Kendrick and me. Victoria's warning kept ringing in my head, as did my assertion that I knew nothing would come of our liaison.

But the truth was that I wanted more. Our brief time together had shown me that being married to him would be no hardship. I now knew I would enjoy the marriage bed as long as I was sharing it with him.

I shivered as I replayed the experience in my mind. I only hoped we'd be able to find a way to be alone together again before the season ended. That he wouldn't grow tired of me too soon and move on to another woman.

I stayed in my happy little bubble for the rest of the day. I'd already turned in for the night when Henry returned, and I was in no mood to speak to him quite yet.

Quite frankly, I didn't care what had happened after I left with Kendrick. I was furious that the two of them had insisted on continuing their foolish scheme just so my brother could gain some of my dowry. I could think of no other reason Henry would insist I marry his friend.

Money was the one thing Henry needed most of all in this world. But he could sell off some of his holdings if he was in such tight constraints. As I lay in bed thinking over the matter, I wondered whether his two estates were entailed. I didn't want to ask him, and I wouldn't bring it up with Auntie. Henry and I were already causing her enough stress. I wouldn't add to it.

Perhaps now Henry would learn to be frugal. Or maybe he would go in search of an heiress to marry. My brother wasn't a cruel man, so I'm sure he would make someone a good enough husband. But I wasn't sure he'd ever care for someone else as much as he cared for himself.

Needling thoughts rose from a small corner of my mind. *What about Kendrick? He's a Legend. They're notorious for their affairs. And there was that gossip-column article about Kendrick and his last mistress…*

I pushed those thoughts aside. Kendrick had been nothing but honest with me. Whoever my brother chose to court when he became desperate enough for money would probably believe he cared for her.

I rolled over and snuggled under the blankets. I was glad to be going to bed early given how little I'd slept last night.

THE NEXT MORNING, when I made my way downstairs for breakfast, my brother was already up. I moved past him to the sideboard. "I'm surprised you're up so early."

He was leaning back in his chair, his arms folded across his chest. "We need to talk about what happened yesterday."

I shook my head, refusing to turn around. "No, we don't. It never should have come to that. What were you thinking, encouraging Penham to fight a duel over me?"

There was a gasp in the entryway, and I turned to see Aunt Augusta standing there, her hand over her mouth. The color had drained from her face.

"Penham fought a duel over you? Was that why you ran out of here so quickly yesterday morning?" She closed her eyes for a moment and shook her head. "Please tell me he didn't challenge Lord Kendrick."

I put down my plate. "I won't lie to you, Auntie."

Henry was glaring at me as though all of this was my fault. "Are you happy now? If you had just accepted the fact that Penham wanted to marry you—"

"Enough," Aunt Augusta said. "This must stop now before your sister is ruined. If anyone finds out about the duel…"

I looked at Henry then back at her.

She turned to the footman in the hallway. "Can you please send someone to fetch a copy of *The Mayfair Chronicle*?"

Now *I* closed my eyes. The gossip column that reported on the Legends—if word had spread about the duel, it would be reported there.

Henry rose from the table and glared at me. "You've always been difficult, acting like the perfect princess who is so above everyone. You've never had to worry about anything in your life."

"Enough, Henry," Aunt Augusta said again.

I stared at my brother, speechless. Was this how he actually saw me? I went out of my way *not* to be a nuisance. It wasn't my fault that I didn't care for all the attention bestowed on me because of my appearance. He'd had everything handed to him when Father died. I wasn't to blame for him gambling away all his money.

I said nothing and just watched him leave the room. Aunt Augusta dropped into the chair he'd vacated. I abandoned the sideboard and sat next to her.

"If it's reported that Kendrick and Lord Penham fought a duel over you, then you'll be ruined," she said, turning to look at me. She cupped my cheek. "You look so much like your mother, and I hate the fact that I've failed her."

I reached up to grasp her hand and pulled it down, squeezing it between both of mine. "It will be fine. I know you only wanted what was best for me, but I never wanted to marry. I'll be able to live on the money I receive from my unused dowry."

Her face was soft as she looked at me. "Of all the men you could have developed feelings for, it had to be a Legend."

I looked away since I couldn't deny it.

She leaned back in her chair. "What are we going to do now?"

I had no idea.

CHAPTER 33

KENDRICK

After leaving Caroline with Moreland's wife, I couldn't stop thinking about her. It baffled me that one woman, above all others, could occupy my thoughts in such a way.

At first, I'd thought perhaps it was her innocence that I found refreshing, but I'd quickly seen that Caroline was mature beyond her years. She was sensible and practical in a way I admired. And despite her lack of experience, she'd shown a depth of passion that had matched mine.

After we'd made love, I'd wondered if she would start making demands on me and my time. But when I'd suggested she return home, she'd readily agreed. For some reason, that didn't sit right with me.

I didn't feel like heading to King's early, so I went back to my townhouse. My steward had been after me to look at some estate matters, and now was as good a time as any. But even when I found myself buried in letters and account books, Caroline was never far from my mind.

I finally understood what was happening after several hours had passed and I was on my way to the club.

I was worried about her.

The realization surprised me. I'd never concerned myself with what women did after they left my bed. I imagined they went about their day just as I went about mine, and I didn't think about them again until I felt another itch for female companionship.

But Caroline had mentioned she would try to make an excuse to stay home tonight, which meant I wouldn't see her again today. That thought shouldn't have bothered me, but it did.

I spent the evening as usual—winning at cards mainly, losing at billiards to Fairfax. The man could never beat Moreland, but he'd improved his skills enough to trounce me routinely.

As I headed home, I had the wayward thought that perhaps I should seek out alternative female companionship. I discarded it immediately, though, since I didn't want to be with anyone else right now. So I went home alone and, after a restless night, returned to King's the following morning.

The club was normally empty during the morning and early afternoon, when men liked to make an appearance at White's or Brooks. They would head to King's later in the evening. It was only midday now, so only the core group of us were there, along with a few others who went out of their way to avoid the other two clubs.

Moreland was there today, and he approached me as soon as I entered the billiard room. I saw the newspaper in his hand and had an uncanny sense of *déjà vu*. Only a few months earlier, I'd shown him that damnable article in *The Mayfair Chronicle* about me wanting to marry my previous mistress. The author had already reported that I was courting the diamond, but now I braced for the worst.

"Please tell me they didn't hear about what happened yesterday."

"I'm afraid so," Moreland said, handing me the paper.

The broadsheet was already open to the page in question. I scanned the gossip column and cursed.

It appears that a certain Legend isn't content to choose his mistresses from the demimonde. Apparently, this gentleman has developed a taste for rarer jewels, and he's recently been reported to have engaged in a duel over her.

The column went on to talk about Fairfax's latest liaison and to speculate on why Clifton, Greyson, and Rexford had been so quiet of late. Although, the author did wonder why we'd all chosen to attend Almack's the other night.

"Well, at least this time she didn't name me. And unlike her last column, she said nothing about the diamond."

"That's hardly a saving grace. Everyone will know she's talking about you because she went on to talk about the rest of us."

"She didn't mention you." I was grasping at straws, and we both knew it.

"I've never had a mistress. It's clear she was talking about you."

I massaged my temples, feeling a headache beginning to form. "What a nightmare."

Moreland leaned against the wall. "No one was surprised by your interest in Miss Edwards. She's beautiful and they've seen you together. But the duel?" He shook his head. "Everyone will be speculating about the reason why you were called out."

I struggled to keep my anger in check. I'd hoped that no one would learn about the duel. Were the servants being paid to share secrets about us? Our carriage drivers? Or the maid Caroline had brought with her then abandoned?

I wanted to call on Caroline, but I didn't know whether it would be wise to add fuel to the fire.

"I must say," Moreland said, "I find it interesting to be on the other side of this situation."

I raised a brow. "The other side?"

He nodded toward the newspaper. "Watching one of you fall under the enchantment of a young woman."

I bristled immediately. "I am not *enchanted* by her."

His gaze was steady. "But you did fight a duel over her."

"Of course. I wasn't about to let Penham gain

the upper hand there. Any of you would have done the same."

"Perhaps," Moreland said. "He always was a bit of a toad at school. And I must say, he hasn't improved with age. But to duel over a woman?"

I stiffened. "You had no problem rushing to a woman's aid when Rexford asked."

Moreland winced. "I have to admit that I was intrigued by her the moment I saw her here that first day."

I said nothing, but I could well understand what Moreland was talking about. I'd felt the same way when I met Caroline. She had a beauty that was unparalleled, but what had struck me most about her was her intelligence. And that she wasn't singularly focused on ensnaring a husband.

"What should I do? I'm not sure it's wise to go to her. But if she's seen this, she will be upset. Perhaps I should stay away from her. Allow time for the speculation to pass." I hated that notion even as the words left my lips.

"Kendrick."

I turned to see that Rexford had approached from the other side. I'd been so intent on what I should do about Caroline that I hadn't noticed him until he was upon us. "I suppose you saw the article."

Rexford nodded. "Yes. And we need to talk."

I narrowed my gaze. He seemed particularly serious today. "About this column?"

"No," Rexford said. "About Miss Edwards. I've been keeping an eye on things after that whole situation unfolded with respect to Weston's actions here that night."

A heavy weight settled in the pit of my stomach. "And?"

Rexford's gaze was unrelenting. "I think Miss Edwards might be in danger."

My alarm intensified. "From whom? Penham?"

"And her brother. Word is it that Weston is growing desperate. He needs his sister to marry Penham."

"Fuck." I was going to kill the two of them.

Moreland clapped me on the shoulder. "Let's go."

I had no idea how I could help, but Rexford wasn't one to overreact. If he thought Caroline was in danger, the threat was real.

I nodded, pleased that I would have Moreland at my side. If a physical altercation broke out, he was the best fighter among us.

CHAPTER 34

CAROLINE

When I couldn't think of a way to distract myself from worrying about my brother and Lord Kendrick, I returned to my room and lay down on the bed. I remained like that for some time, trying to quiet my racing thoughts. But instead of falling asleep, I kept replaying Henry's parting words. I didn't know how much time had passed when a maid knocked at the door to tell me I had a caller.

I stood and smoothed out my skirts. A quick glance at the dressing table mirror told me my hair didn't need to be redone. I took a deep breath and made my way downstairs.

I was hoping Kendrick had called, but to my disappointment, Henry and Penham were waiting in the drawing room. I'd hoped losing the duel to Kendrick would have kept Penham away. But aside from his right arm being cradled against his chest in a sling, he didn't appear to be suffering any ill effects.

I hesitated in the doorway, but when they both turned to look at me, I knew it was too late to escape. "I was told that I had a caller." I turned to look at my brother. "Perhaps Aunt Augusta should be here for this meeting."

Henry stood with his hands on his hips. "She's gone out. But don't worry, I'm here to guard your virtue."

There was an odd note in his voice when he said that last word, and I wondered whether he suspected what had happened when I'd left the dueling field with Kendrick. I couldn't help but feel a thread of alarm at this confrontation, but I refused to give them the upper hand. I walked into the room, hands folded at my waist, and waited for them to speak. We stood like that for an uncomfortably long time before Penham spoke.

"Weston and I have come to an agreement," he said. "I am having my solicitors draw up the marriage agreement, and we will be married shortly."

I froze in place, unable to believe what I was hearing.

Henry added, "I thought it best to let you know what was happening so you could have a little bit of time to get used to the idea. But this is going to happen, Caroline."

I shook my head. "I don't agree to this. You can't force me."

Henry's eyes narrowed. "What are you going to do if I decide to cut you off? You can't marry anyone else without my permission, and you have no money."

"I can stay with Auntie."

He made a small dismissive snort. "Who do you think has been paying her bills?"

That information surprised me. "But she is a widow. She has money that was settled upon her, and the dower house at Lord Fredricks's estate."

Henry shook his head. "The dower house is hers, yes, but it is currently undergoing repairs. Apparently, her husband let it fall into an abysmal state. I have been paying her living expenses until that is done. And since money is tight, I've decided to stop doing that."

"That is cruel, even for you, Henry."

He shrugged. "It is not actually my responsibility to see to her living expenses. The new Lord Fredricks should be doing that, but he is a miserly fellow who has all but washed his hands of her."

Holding out for my own independence was one thing. I knew I would have an adequate amount of money settled upon me when the money set aside for my dowry came to me. But I'd had no idea my refusal to marry could hurt Aunt Augusta.

I stared at Henry. "How could you do this?"

"You've left me no choice. You could have married a wealthy man. You could have married Penham last year. But instead, you decided to indulge a man who is known to keep mistresses and who will never marry you."

I latched onto the anger that sparked within me at his dismissive words. "Lord Kendrick is far more honorable than the two of you. He would never force a woman to do something that she didn't want to do."

Penham snorted at that. "I'm sure all the women he's bedded wouldn't agree."

I laughed. "I can assure you, my lord, that every

woman who has been with Kendrick has been fully satisfied with their arrangement."

Penham froze, his mouth tightening and his face mottling with rage. "What do you know about it?" He took a menacing step forward, and I held my ground.

"Caroline," Henry said, "tell me that you are not one of those women."

I hesitated, the truth warring with my sense of self-preservation.

Then Penham turned to Henry. "This wasn't part of our agreement. You assured me that she would be untouched."

A spark of hope flared to life within me. But I chose to remain silent since the two men were now facing each other.

"She's lying." Henry glanced over at me but then turned back to look at Penham. "She is only saying this because she's hoping that you'll change your mind." Penham stared silently at me, and Henry continued. "I think it's time that we quit London. She has spent far too much time in Kendrick's company. I'll take her home, and you can marry her there."

I shook my head and took a step backward, surprised when my body collided with another. I whirled around to find Kendrick standing in the doorway. I hadn't even heard him knock on the front door. Baron Moreland moved into place next to him, and the two of them made a formidable pair.

I looked between them and my brother and Lord Penham, who were standing in the middle of the drawing room, and decided to stay with the two Legends. How ironic that I felt safer with these two men—whom society had renounced as irreparable rogues—than with my own brother and his closest friend.

Kendrick looked down at me. "It seems you have a decision to make, Caroline. Are you returning to the country with your brother and his *friend*?" His voice dripped with scorn on that last word. "Or would you rather remain in London with me?"

I had only one answer to that. "I'm going to stay."

Henry stepped forward. "Not without my permission, you're not."

Kendrick moved to stand in front of me, and Moreland winked at me before taking his place at Kendrick's side. Together, they formed a very effective wall between my brother and me.

"I have a promissory note that says otherwise," Kendrick said. "You gave her into my care, and I have witnesses who can corroborate that."

"Tell me," Moreland said, "do you want to be known as the man who gave away his sister in a card game?"

Henry was shaking his head. "You wouldn't dare."

Kendrick laughed. "Of course I would."

"But she'll be ruined," Penham said.

Kendrick and Moreland looked at one another, and Kendrick smiled. "Like Moreland's wife was ruined?"

We'd all heard the rumors about what had happened at the beginning of the season. I knew that those rumors were true, but society had forgiven everything when Moreland and Victoria wed.

They'd quickly moved on to other topics. Right now, the gossip was the scandal surrounding me. But in a month's time, another scandal would take its place, and people would forget about me. I would still be ruined, but since I hadn't wanted to marry anyway, I didn't care.

Kendrick examined his nails. "How many duels

do I have to win? Maybe next time my aim will be truer."

Penham's hands went up in the air, and he turned to my brother. "I'm done with this. Your sister is not worth this trouble. There are more than enough beautiful young women who are amenable to being told what they should do. You'll have to find someone else to fix the mess you've made of your finances."

"That sounds about right," Kendrick said as Penham brushed past him. "You always were one to give up when faced with a challenge."

Penham said nothing as he stormed from the house.

Henry stood there, staring at us. Then muttering a curse, he went after his friend.

Silence settled in the room. Kendrick and I were staring at one another, and I had almost forgotten that Moreland was there until he murmured something about waiting for Kendrick outside to make sure we weren't interrupted. Then he was gone, and it was just the two of us.

CHAPTER 35

KENDRICK

Caroline and I stared at each other for several seconds, then she wrapped her arms around her waist and folded in on herself. I took a step toward her, wanting to draw her into my arms, but she shook her head.

"There's something I need to give you," she said. "I'll go fetch it now." She didn't wait for my agreement before turning and heading upstairs.

I paced while I waited, hating that she'd pushed me away when all I wanted was to take her into my arms and offer her comfort. She wasn't gone for long, five minutes perhaps, before she came downstairs again. I was waiting at the base of the stairs and saw that she held a piece of paper.

She passed me, and I followed her into the drawing room. The tense atmosphere set my nerves on edge. Caroline's shoulders were pulled back, and her rigid posture told me that she was summoning the strength to say something.

"You can tell me anything," I said, aching to wipe away the small furrow between her brows.

Caroline blew out her breath and met my gaze. "I apologize for all the trouble I've been to you."

I raised a brow. "You've done nothing wrong. It was your brother who set all of this in motion."

She gave a small laugh at that. "Yes, well, I suppose he's regretting that decision. At any rate, I know I've asked much of you, and I appreciate the fact that you've been a staunch ally in all this. But I've come to the realization that I've behaved self-ishly in imposing on your kindness."

I frowned. "My kindness? Do you think I've been acting out of a sense of kind-heartedness?" I hadn't meant to sound quite so annoyed, but she clearly picked up on it.

"I don't blame you for being angry. When you came here that first morning, you wanted nothing to do with this, and it was my idea to ask you to pretend an interest in me you weren't feeling."

I shook my head. "Tell me, Caroline. Do you think that everything that's passed between us has been pretend?"

She flushed. She was surely thinking about the intimacies we'd shared.

"I know I am not special to you."

I wanted to protest, but something in her face had me holding still. She held out the paper, and I took it automatically.

I unfolded the note and scanned the lines. Disbelief crashed through me. "What is this?"

"It is a promissory note. You can add it to the one my brother gave you. I give you my word that when I receive my dowry, I will give you the amount Henry owes. I am, of course, willing to add interest, as well as whatever you think would be a fair recompense for all the trouble you've gone through on my behalf."

I couldn't hold back my bitter laugh. "I am not in the habit of being paid to bed women."

She flinched at the words. "I was referring to the duel, but as for that…"

I waited, but she looked away.

"Enough," she said softly to herself. Then she

met my gaze again. "Perhaps one day, when we cross paths, we can do so on less tumultuous terms. I would love to consider you a friend, but I free you from any sense of responsibility you might feel toward me. I have demanded too much of your time already."

She nodded then turned to leave. I watched her go, frozen in place. I didn't know how much time passed as I stood there, but I did hear her footsteps on the stairs. Finally, my emotions in turmoil, I strode from the house.

Moreland was waiting outside. He frowned when he saw me. "What happened?"

I still held the promissory note, and I gave it to him.

He read it then handed it back to me. "You seem to be collecting a fair number of these."

"Indeed." A hollow pit had opened inside me, and it was impossible to think.

"So, what does this mean?"

"It means that she's given me my freedom. She doesn't expect me to pretend that I'm courting her."

Moreland shifted, but his face took on an amused smirk. "So you're free of the whole ordeal. What do you plan to do now?"

I scowled, annoyed by his reaction.

Moreland watched me. "You don't seem relieved."

I started to massage my chest. Why did I feel as though I'd been punched there? "I should be."

Moreland's eyes narrowed as he continued to examine me. "What is the matter?"

I turned to look back at the townhouse. "I'm worried about what's going to happen to her now. Her brother has threatened to take her away from London, and I know that he still wants to marry her off."

I couldn't help thinking about all the men who would love to marry Caroline. All they wanted was someone young and beautiful. They would squash her spirit, and she would have to hide her intelligence. I wanted to call them out right now. Every single person who'd ever looked at her with interest, especially those who had ever dared call on her.

"Well, that's not your problem now," Moreland said.

I turned back to him, aghast.

He was smiling now. "You're not going to miss her, are you? Did you at least get to bed her?"

I didn't hold back. I punched him and, for some reason, was breathing heavily.

Moreland massaged his jaw. "I'll allow that, but only once because I've never seen a bigger idiot in my life."

My fists were still clenched, but I managed to hold back from hitting him again. Despite what he'd said, I knew he'd allow it.

Moreland shook his head. "You're in love with her, you daft fool."

I froze, staring at him for several long seconds before turning back to look at the house. Is that what this feeling was? The dread that had settled over me when she'd handed me that damned promissory note? The certainty that I wouldn't know what to do with myself tomorrow if I couldn't see her again?

"What are you going to do about it?" Moreland said. "Are you going to let her go? Allow someone else to steal her away?"

My chest had become almost unbearably tight.

Moreland clapped me on the shoulder. "You love her, Kendrick. If you let her go, you will regret it forever."

The certainty in his voice shook me out of my confusion because he was correct. I was already regretting that I hadn't stopped her from walking away. I should have snatched her back. I should have raced up those stairs, found her bedroom, and told her I was never going to let her go.

I turned to look at Moreland.

He was grinning. "It seems that we're both fools."

I closed my eyes for a moment, recognizing the truth of his words. But I was already beginning to feel lighter. "Thank you for everything. I'll see you later."

I turned and headed back into the townhouse. The footman in the front hallway was startled to see me.

"Where is her bedroom?" I demanded.

He stiffened. "I'm afraid I cannot—"

"I give you my word that I won't debauch her under your roof, but I do need to speak to her right away."

I should have been annoyed that he so easily gave me instructions on where to find her. I took the stairs two at a time, worrying whether he'd do the same for the next man who came here looking for Caroline. I needed to get to her as soon as possible and straighten out this mess.

I knocked when I reached the room the footman had told me was hers, but not because I needed permission. I knocked because all of this would be over before it started if Lady Fredricks was home and the man had sent me to her bedroom instead of Caroline's.

"Not now."

My chest tightened again when I heard her muffled voice. She was crying. I flung open the door and stood there. She lay curled on her crumpled bed, her face buried in the bedspread.

"I said not now, Henry. I can't deal with you right now."

"It's me."

Her entire body stiffened, then she turned to look at me. Her eyes widened, and she hurried to stand, wobbling a little on her feet.

"What are you doing here?" Her gaze went to the open door.

I turned and closed it.

"You can't be here," she said with a frown. "Was the note not enough? Did I not do it correctly?"

I was still holding that damned promissory note in my hands, but I'd crumpled it into a ball. I lifted it, straightened the paper, and tore it in two. "I can't accept this. I was never going to accept your money. I want the diamond I was promised."

Her breath hitched. "I don't understand."

I took a step closer. "Neither do I, but it appears that I've come to think of you as mine. No one else can have you."

Her frown deepened. "I am not an object to be given away—"

"I love you, Caroline."

She froze and stared at me. "What did you say?"

I smiled and moved closer. When I finally reached her, I cupped her cheek and stared down at the most beautiful woman I'd ever known.

"You are, without a doubt, the largest thorn in my side, but I cannot imagine my life without you."

Then I did something I had never expected to do. I dropped down onto one knee. "Caroline Edwards, will you do me the honor of becoming my wife?"

She gasped then pulled me up before flinging herself into my arms. "Yes," she said, her voice shaking, this time with something other than sadness. "Yes, a million times, yes."

I held her like that, gathered to me. I half expected to feel constriction in my chest again, but instead I was filled with a sense of buoyancy. I stared down at her, cognizant of the fact that I was grinning like a fool. "I thought you didn't want to marry anyone."

"I could say the same thing about you."

I raised a brow and waited.

"Fine, we've both been stubborn. But I love you, too, Kendrick. I didn't want to admit it, but I've known almost since the beginning that you are the only man I could ever see myself consenting to marry."

I kissed her then, before the footman could assemble an army of servants to tear me from Caroline's side.

EPILOGUE

CAROLINE

We set the wedding date for the end of the season, which meant we had three weeks of hurried preparations. After news of the duel had spread throughout the ton, Auntie refused to hear anything about us getting a special license and marrying quickly. When she'd come home that day to learn that Kendrick and I were engaged, she chose to overlook the fact that she'd found us in my bedroom. We were both fully clothed, so she could pretend that nothing untoward had happened.

Henry had no choice but to give his consent for

the betrothal, but he made it a point to be absent whenever Kendrick called. I no longer had to endure Penham's visits, thank heavens, and his friendship with my brother had cooled considerably. I couldn't say I was sorry to hear that. I had no proof, but I'd come to suspect that he'd encouraged my brother's worst excesses.

For the most part, Auntie kept me busy with the wedding preparations. But now that it was only a few days before the wedding and most of the arrangements were in place, including my wedding dress and the invitations that had gone out to only a few select members of the ton, she turned her attention to ensuring that Kendrick was never alone with me. She wisely decided he could not be trusted.

After a great deal of convincing, I obtained her permission to call on Victoria that afternoon. I was hoping Kendrick would also be there and that we'd be able to slip away for a few minutes of privacy. When I'd mentioned the visit to him yesterday, he'd been evasive. I knew he wasn't having second thoughts about our marriage, but I couldn't help thinking he was holding something back from me.

Victoria was waiting for me in the drawing room, and she rose to give me a quick hug. "This is so exciting. I feel bad for telling you Kendrick wouldn't marry you. I was certain he was going to break your heart."

Her exuberance almost matched mine. "I'm so glad you were wrong."

"Come with me. I have something to show you." She had a twinkle in her eye that I hoped meant Kendrick was waiting for me in another room.

I followed her to the dining room, and my eyes fell on my soon-to-be husband, who was standing just inside the doorway. My spirits soared, as it always did whenever I saw him. Only when he shifted to one side did I see the other Legends standing on the far end of the room.

I watched in shock as they all raised a glass to me.

I turned to Kendrick "What is happening?"

He dropped a kiss on my cheek. "We're officially welcoming you into the Legends."

I stared at him. Surely I'd misheard. Victoria had been welcomed into their group, but she was Rexford's sister, after all. I never imagined they'd extend the same welcome to me.

Rexford approached and bowed. I'd never spoken to him before, but there was no mistaking him. He was almost as attractive as Kendrick, and I was fairly certain that half the women of the ton, married and unmarried, were in love with him. "This is for you."

I took the coin he held out. "What is this?" Confused, I looked down at it and gasped when I realized what I was holding.

On one side of the coin was a six-pointed star, symbolizing the six Legends. On the other was the crown that symbolized Rexford's club, King's. I stared at him. "Is this what I think it is?"

He smiled. "Welcome to the Legends. Try to keep this one in check," he said, nodding toward Kendrick.

Fondness unfurled within me. Something about this man had me wanting to please him. He'd brought together these six men, and they'd formed a tight-knit bond that was stronger than those found in most families. They would do anything for one another, and that included welcoming the women they married.

I turned to where Victoria had moved to stand next to her husband, grinning. "I can't believe this is happening." I looked at Kendrick, then Rexford again. "My brother is going to be furious when he learns of this."

We all laughed, and I felt a lightness in my chest. Henry would never be welcome at King's again. And while I wasn't foolish enough to think I could come and go as I pleased—it was still a gentleman's club, after all—this coin represented something even better. I was marrying a Legend and was welcome within their group. Only two women had managed to accomplish that feat.

Everyone raised their glasses, and Fairfax stepped forward. "To Miss Caroline Edwards. The diamond Kendrick never wanted but couldn't give up."

I joined in their laughter and took the glass of champagne Victoria handed me. Then I raised it to make my own toast. "To the brothers who've proven to be more accepting than my own." They began to raise their glasses again until I added, "And to the women you will all one day marry."

A twinkle of amusement glinted in Rexford's eyes, but Clifton, Greyson, and Fairfax all seemed appalled. Victoria and I burst into giggles and drank heartily from our champagne. Moreland and Kendrick didn't laugh, but I could tell they were also amused.

I turned to Kendrick while the others descended on the food laid out on the dining room sideboard.

"Only three days until the wedding. I almost couldn't convince Auntie to allow me to visit today. I think she might lock me in my room when she learns I've been with a group of known rogues."

He smiled down at me. "I'll scale the wall to your bedroom."

I laughed, wrapping my arms around his neck. "That won't be necessary. I'll make sure to sneak downstairs and leave the side door open for you."

He pulled me closer. "Three more days, and then you'll be mine."

"I was yours the day you showed up in my drawing room with that promissory note."

EPILOGUE 2

THE MAYFAIR CHRONICLE

Lady X

Two Legends have fallen.

*With the recent news about Lord Kendrick and Miss Caro-
line Edwards's engagement, the others should watch their
backs. Now that it's been revealed that miracles can happen
more than once, I suspect that mothers will no longer be
ushering their daughters in a different direction when they spot
one of these renowned rakes.*

*There is a rumor, after all, that rakes do make the best
husbands… If you can manage to entice one, that is.*

Thank you for reading WON BY THE VISCOUNT! I had so much fun writing this story and I hope you enjoyed reading it.

Did you miss Moreland and Victoria's story? RUINED BY THE BARON is out now. Turn the page for an excerpt from their book.

TAKEN BY THE EARL will be book 3 in the Legendary Lords of the Ton series. It will tell the Earl of Clifton and Miss Diana Atherton's story.

And don't forget to join my mailing list to be among the first to learn when I have a new book available and to receive bonus content! Join today at suzannamedeiros.com/newsletter

EXCERPT—RUINED BY THE BARON

"Sit down, Victoria."

He'd called me Victoria, not Lady Victoria. If his goal was to shock me into silence, it worked. I lowered myself onto the edge of the settee and waited for him to settle into one of the two armchairs placed across from where I sat. Instead, he sank onto the settee next to me.

He'd left space between us, but nothing about sitting this close to an unmarried man could be called respectable—a handsome man who was filled with vitality and to whom I was very much attracted. An image popped into my mind that threatened to steal my breath. Moreland leaning toward me, closing that negligible amount of space, and pressing his mouth against mine.

"I apologize for distressing you just now."

The image faded, and for a disorienting moment, I couldn't remember to what he was referring. "Your news," I said finally.

His gaze hadn't left mine, and it felt as though he was trying to see right through me.

"I've learned that news of our arrangement has made it into the gossip columns."

I gasped. "Which ones?"

His brows drew together. "I was told the news secondhand. Why?"

My heart raced in earnest. "Father reads *The Mayfair Chronicle*."

"Of course he does." Moreland rolled his eyes.

We both knew why Father chose to read the gossip column in that particular newspaper. He hated that Rexford had escaped his control and was obsessed with any news related to his son. *The Mayfair Chronicle* had taken a particular interest in Rexford, giving his circle of friends the moniker by which everyone now knew them. The Legendary Lords of the ton.

Every time Father read that paper, his mood soured. And since news about their exploits was an almost daily event, he was always in a foul mood.

He would be apoplectic with rage when he

learned that I was being kept as one of their mistresses. It also meant that Moreland's life could be in danger. That distressing thought hadn't occurred to me until that moment.

"We need to stop this. I should have taken up Rexford's offer to hide me away in the country."

Moreland shook his head. "We've already discussed this. We both know that your father could explain away your sudden absence. Manufacture a family emergency while he turned England upside down looking for you."

I closed my eyes, but I couldn't deny the truth of Moreland's words.

"And when he found you, he would continue with his plans undeterred."

After I'd had a chance to recover from the beating he would no doubt give me. But he would be careful not to mar my face or arms. He wouldn't want to damage the property he intended to barter for a powerful alliance. But he would have no such qualms when it came to Moreland.

"I'm afraid for your safety."

He barked out a laugh, and I wanted to shake him.

Can't he see that he's in danger?

"Victoria—"

"You're not safe. You might think you are because Father has done nothing to hurt Rexford. But my brother is his heir. Father labors under the mistaken impression that he can still bring him to heel. But you… He would have no misgivings about doing whatever was necessary to hurt the man who dared to impugn the family's honor."

His face softened. "Not your honor?"

This time I laughed. "*His* honor. We are but walking, talking extensions of his name. Rexford has some leeway because he is a man. Men are allowed to sow their oats, get into all manner of scrapes in their youth, but all is forgiven when they wish to return to the fold."

Moreland shook his head. "Rexford will never return to the fold."

"Perhaps not, but he will become the next Duke of Sherbourne. And no one will care what he did before that time—or after, for that matter. He has full impunity. But me?" With each word, I became more convinced about the futility of this whole exercise. "Father will have you killed for trying to ruin me and thwart his plans."

"He can try, but I'm an excellent shot. And I can hold my own with a blade."

This time, I feared my laughter held more than

a hint of hysteria. "You think he'll call you out? No, there are other ways to take a man's life." I'd read more than a few horrid novels, and in that moment, I could recall every ghastly death that had befallen those who'd wandered into the wrong place at the wrong time.

"Victoria—"

"No, we must stop this now. There's still time if our names weren't mentioned…"

My protests died when Moreland placed his hands on my cheeks and physically turned me to face him. We remained like that for what seemed like an eternity, his hands cupping my face and our thighs pressed together.

I already knew that his eyes were a light gray—it was impossible not to notice such an uncommon color. But now I could see that darker flecks swirled within them. And as we continued to stare at each other, I could see the way his pupils grew larger. If I were capable of speech, I would have asked him why. It seemed like such an odd thing to notice, but I couldn't help but wonder if something significant was happening between us.

Surely I was imagining things, but the very air that surrounded us seemed to grow thick with tension.

"I'm going to take care of you."

A soft whimper escaped, and I wanted to sink through the floor. *What is wrong with me?*

But the sound seemed to bring about a strange reaction in Moreland. His lids grew heavy, and his face came closer.

The sharp knock at the front door sent both of us scrambling backward.

© Suzanna Medeiros

ABOUT SUZANNA

USA Today bestselling author Suzanna Medeiros was born and raised in Toronto, Canada. Her love for the written word led her to pursue a degree in English Literature from the University of Toronto. She went on to earn a Bachelor of Education degree before deciding to pursue her first love—writing.

Suzanna is married to her own hero and survived raising twins. When she isn't writing she loves reading, watching science fiction, and playing video games.

She would like to thank her parents for showing her that love at first sight and happily ever after really do exist.

To learn more about Suzanna's books, you can visit her website at www.suzannamedeiros.com.

To learn when she has a new release available, you can sign up for her mailing list at suzannamedeiros.com/newsletter.

instagram.com/suzannamedeiros
facebook.com/AuthorSuzannaMedeiros

BOOKS BY SUZANNA MEDEIROS

Legendary Lords of the Ton series:

Ruined by the Baron

Won by the Viscount

Taken by the Earl (coming next)

Landing a Lord series:

Dancing with the Duke

Loving the Marquess

Beguiling the Earl

The Unaffected Earl

The Unsuitable Duke

The Unexpected Marquess

The Unwilling Viscount

The Baron's Return

Courting the Earl

Tempting the Viscount

Christmas Scandals series:

A Viscount for Christmas

A Highwayman for Christmas

A Rogue for Christmas

A Betrothal for Christmas (coming soon)

Hathaway Heirs series:

Lady Hathaway's Proposal

Lord Hathaway's Bride

Captain Hathaway's Dilemma

Miss Hathaway's Wish

Single Titles:

Dear Stranger

Forbidden in February

Anthologies:

The Novellas: A Collection

Hathaway Heirs: Books 1-4

Landing a Lord: Books 1-3

Landing a Lord: Books 4-6

Landing a Lord: Books 7-9

Christmas Scandals: Books 1-3

For more information and an up-to-date book list please
visit the author's website: suzannamedeiros.com/books